POLARIS

ALSO BY MICHAEL NORTHROP

Gentlemen

Trapped

Plunked

Rotten

Surrounded by Sharks

The TombQuest *Series*

POLARIS

MICHAEL NORTHROP

SCHOLASTIC PRESS

NEW YORK

Library of Congress Cataloging-in-Publication Data
Names: Northrop, Michael, author.
Title: Polaris / Michael Northrop.
Description: First edition. | New York : Scholastic Press, 2017. | Summary: In the 1830s
Owen Ward is cabin boy on the *Polaris*, a ship on a voyage of scientific exploration,
when illness and a mutiny off the coast of Brazil cause the adult crew to abandon the
ship, leaving the handful of young cabin attendants and deckhands behind. The young
seafarers are determined to bring their ship to safety, but when one of them disappears
they begin to suspect that there is something deadly on board with them.
Identifiers: LCCN 2016059059 | ISBN 9780545297165 (hc)
Subjects: LCSH: Seafaring life—Juvenile fiction. | Ships—Juvenile fiction. | Sea stories. |
Adventure stories. | CYAC: Seafaring life—Fiction. | Ships—Fiction. | Adventure and
adventurers—Fiction.
Classification: LCC PZ7.N8185 Po 2017 | DDC [Fic]—dc23
LC record available at https://lccn.loc.gov/2016059059

10 9 8 7 6 5 4 3 2 1   17 18 19 20 21

Printed in the U.S.A.   23
First edition, November 2017

Map by Jim McMahon
Book design by Phil Falco

FOR MY DAD, LARRY,
WHO HAD THAT AMAZING, ICONIC *JAWS* MOVIE
POSTER IN HIS OFFICE WHEN I WAS A KID.
THAT WAS MY FIRST TASTE OF HOW
TANTALIZINGLY SCARY THE SEA COULD BE.
AND OF COURSE IT WAS ALSO THE MOVIE
THAT TAUGHT ME THAT, SOMETIMES,
WE ALL NEED A BIGGER BOAT.

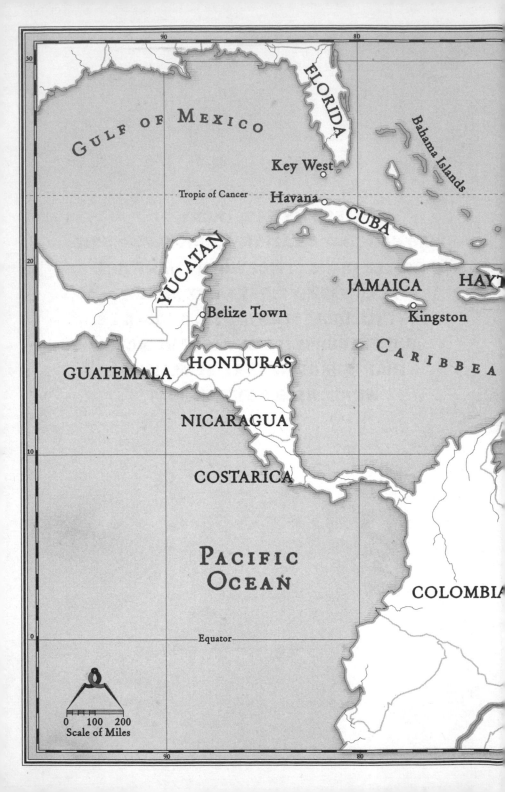

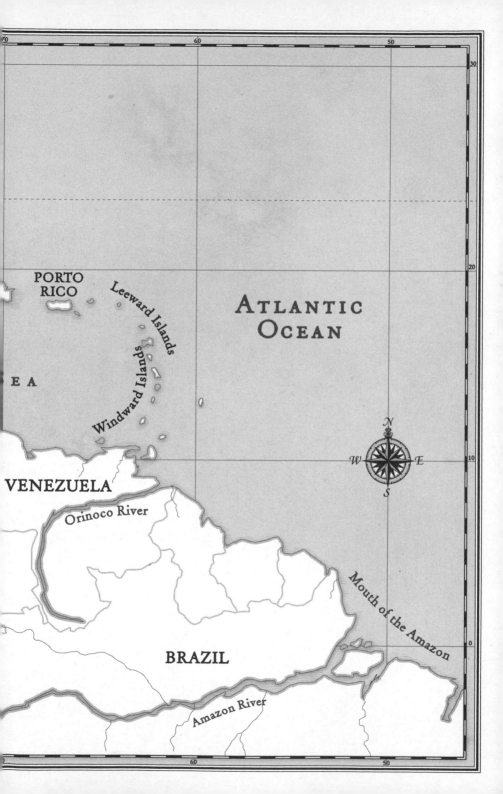

IT BEGINS

The 1830s, somewhere off the coast of Brazil

The proud sailing ship *Polaris* bobbed up and down on the waves as it lay at anchor. Just across the surf sprawled the massive, teeming Amazon rain forest. Cabin boy Owen Ward stood at the ship's rail, peering at the river mouth through a borrowed spyglass. He watched the soft flow of muddy river water emptying into the somber, salty Atlantic.

As a passing swell lifted the ship's wooden hull, his view shifted. He saw the greens and browns of towering trees and winding vines, and the deep shadows beneath them that hid all manner of unimaginable wildlife. Even a quarter mile out and above the murmur of the surf, he could hear a nonstop chorus of caws and shrieks and chirps emanating from the jungle. What he could neither see nor hear, though, was any sign of the ship's launch, the long, sturdy rowboat that had ferried the shore party to their mission.

The launch had disappeared up the murky river more than a week earlier, carrying with it the ship's captain, first mate, doctor, and eight of its best sailors, along with the strange fellow who had necessitated this trip in the first place. Owen tried to remember the word . . . "botanist"—that was it. A man in the philosophical line who studied flowers and trees and such, if he understood correctly.

Owen lowered the glass, collapsing the two brass tubes into each other and sheathing the device in the one large pocket of his ragged black vest. He wore the vest open, the buttons a distant memory, over a threadbare shirt. His pants were duck canvas trousers worn in the sailor's fashion: tight around the hips and long and flowing around the ankles. His shoes weren't there at all.

The *Polaris* was here on a scientific expedition—"a voyage of discovery," the captain had called it. Now Owen looked around the deck at the rear end of that voyage. There were a dozen men, not the best of the crew so much as the rest of the crew. Scattered among them were half as many ship's boys, who worked cheaper, ate less, and took up less space. Owen knew well that a boat without its captain was an empty and idle thing, and when the first mate was gone too . . .

A few of the men halfheartedly pushed mops around the deck. A few more kept questionable watch up in the rigging with eyes half-closed. Others busied themselves with not being busy. Several sailors lounged openly about the elevated forecastle at the front of the ship, as if passing a lazy Sunday after a week of hard sailing. But there had been no sailing at all this week, only waiting. The lone exception: The third mate had sent a ship's boy named Manny aloft to apply a protective coating of grease to the mainmast, perhaps hoping to set a good example. It hadn't worked.

Owen hovered near the back of the ship, away from the rest. He was not quite thirteen years old, though the entry next to his name in the ship's roll read *fifteen*. In his defense, the other ship's boys had all lied about their ages too—it was a proud nautical tradition. And while that ragged lot had the advantage of anonymity, with nothing but their willingness to work hard for a pittance to recommend them for a life at sea, Owen had another time-honored advantage. The captain was his uncle. He was sure the other sailors, the "old salts" and "jack-tars," distrusted him for it. And maybe disliked him too.

That didn't matter at all when his uncle was around. But now, with his uncle and his most trusted men ashore, Owen stayed close to the ship's small quarterdeck. The raised section at the back of the boat was home to the captain's cabin, the ship's large wooden-spoked steering wheel, and a short stretch of deck that was the exclusive domain of the officers. Even with the captain and first mate gone, the sailors dared not go there, for fear of having their sunburned hides whipped bloody. Owen himself was not quite standing on it now, though he was the cabin boy and crossed that rarefied stretch of deck often in his line of work.

In fact, there was only one person standing on the quarterdeck at the moment. It was not the gloomy second mate, William Shannahan, who had gone below deck again for some unfathomable reason. It was a boy no older than Owen, who simply knew no better. Henry Neap was the botanist's assistant, but the captain had deemed him too frail for the inland expedition. Owen glanced over at the boy with open disdain. What he saw was a landlubber of the first order, with not a sailor's bone in his scrawny body, leaning over the railing like a dog awaiting its master. It did not occur to Owen that he was doing much the same thing, as he once again pulled the spyglass from his vest, unfolded the little telescope, and pressed it to his eye.

This time, at long last, he saw what he was looking for. He lowered the glass and raised his voice. "Boat ho!" he cried in the manliest baritone he could muster.

Atop the mainmast high above him, the lookout climbed to his feet. A moment later, he echoed the call. The launch was returning. Down on the deck, the idlers sprang to their feet, and the second mate bolted out of the aft hatch as if shot from it.

"Give me the glass, boy," he said, showing Owen his upturned palm.

"There's something wrong," said Owen, reluctantly handing it over.

Shannahan took a moment to locate the boat in the narrow

4

eye of the lens. "But where are they?" he mumbled. "Where are the rest?"

Owen squinted into the distance. Even without the glass, he could see the trouble: The little boat was half-empty. Where were the other men?

Owen stared at the approaching boat as it crested a breaking wave. Its occupants were shrunk to doll size by distance and bent double over the oars, pulling hard to escape the surf. He scanned the figures, searching desperately for any sign of the captain. Mercifully, he wasn't hard to spot. He was the only one not rowing.

But what of the others? What had happened to them?

As if in answer, the piercing shriek of some wild beast carried across the water. It sounded, to Owen's untrained ear, like wild laughter. And though the day was bright and the sun blistering, a cold shiver shot through him.

In the minutes leading up to the boat's reappearance, Henry Neap had been leaning uneasily over the rail and peering longingly toward land. He was no sailor. He was a botanist's assistant, and he was that to the core. He was gazing out at the tall trees rising from the banks of the river and trying to identify them.

His eye went to the tallest one, towering over the shoreline even at this distance, its green halo dotted with pinprick white flowers. *A kapok tree*, thought Henry, though the scientific name escaped him.

He wished once again that Dr. Wetherby had left his books behind—but much more than that, he wished that the doctor had not left *him* behind! His head drooped in despair. His eyes slid from the dizzying variety of the jungle's edge to the ocean below. He watched the water flop and slop against the side of the ship. He could hardly believe that he'd sailed all this way only to be left behind. He could still hear the captain's words clearly: "Not the boy. Just look at him. These wilds are unexplored, and Lord knows what dangers lurk within, what manner of beasts. This is an expedition for strong men—well, for strong men and *you*, Doctor."

In one harangue, Captain Eagling had managed to insult both Henry and his employer. "Just look at him . . ." Henry stared down at his own soft hands and scrawny arms. As always, it was the truth that stung the most. And now that the expedition was ashore, he knew that he would get no closer to the wild abundance of species that lay just across the water.

Henry looked up again at the treetops swaying lightly in the breeze as if waving him good-bye. So many varieties, one next to the other, but how could he hope to make out the smaller ones at this distance? He glanced over at the cabin boy, who stood a dozen feet away, scanning the shoreline through a spyglass. Henry desperately wanted to borrow it, but he was sure he'd receive nothing more than a punch in the shoulder if he asked. He'd known boys like this one back at school, brawny and athletic. Before Dr. Wetherby had plucked Henry from the head of his class for a life of science, he'd felt the sickening thump of their knuckles driven into his gut many times.

Suddenly, the cabin boy lowered the spyglass and called out, "Boat ho!"

Henry searched the waves, and there it was. The sturdy old rowboat the expedition had taken ashore scaled the face of a breaking wave and then rode swiftly down its back. He scanned the figures, desperate for any sign of the doctor.

He squinted hard, and when that didn't work, he opened his eyes as wide as they would go. Even at this distance, he could see that there were far fewer men returning than had left..He gave up on the tiny faces and searched for the doctor's silver hair or brown jacket. Nothing. Where was he? He cast his eyes back toward shore, hoping to see a campfire or a pitched tent. Perhaps they were just returning for more supplies . . . But there was no sign of the rest of the crew.

A terrible wail carried across the water. Henry's mind told him it was the call of a howling monkey, an exotic beast with a cry reputed to carry for miles. But his gut insisted it was something worse. He looked at the men in the boat, hunched over and pulling desperately on their oars. He heard the wild cry of the jungle behind them. And in that instant he knew it: The expedition wasn't resupplying. It was retreating.

With every stroke, the launch grew closer and larger and clearer. He could see the survivors' torn clothing and dirt-smeared skin. There was no denying it anymore. The doctor was not among them. Henry's head swam, and he had to grip the rail hard just to stay upright.

Is he gone for good? thought Henry. *And am I, once again, alone in this world?*

The mainmast was like a tall, skinny tree shooting skyward, sprouting yardarms instead of branches and clothed in sails instead of leaves. Manny Iglesias was halfway up, swaying from side to side as the ship rolled on the waves, with a bucket of stinking grease in one hand and a brush in the other. That left Manny, short for Manuel, exactly zero hands to hold on to anything but hope. Ship's boys were listed last in the muster book and fed last at mealtime, but theirs were always the first names called for nasty work like greasing the mast. Manny gripped the rope rigging with bare, calloused feet, leaned forward, and said a little prayer. *"Padre nuestro, que estás en el cielo . . ."*

The ship rolled, the mast swayed, and Manny applied another brushful of rotting animal fat to the old wood in the hope that it wouldn't crack in half before the journey was over. The call of "Boat ho!" floated up like a prayer answered.

Manny dropped the brush into the bucket and watched with great interest as the boat approached. A quick count revealed six people, half the number there should have been. A scan of the shore revealed no camp, no one waiting. This was bad.

The second mate reappeared on deck and immediately called, "All hands!" A rush of sailors headed for the rail. Manny hooked the bucket handle under an elbow and scrambled down the horizontal rope ratlines to join them.

The launch covered the distance quickly. "Hoist us aboard, blast you!" called the captain as the boat bobbed perilously close to the heavy wooden sides of the rocking ship. A charge surged through the entire crew at the sound of the captain's voice. Lines were lowered from the boom, and both men and boat were hauled aboard quickly.

Small and slight, Manny was a better fit for work aloft than for hauling—but then, there wasn't much to haul this time. Most of the landing party's equipment and supplies seemed to have been left behind, along with the missing crew.

A thought bubbled to the surface as Manny watched the remaining men scramble over the rail. They left the jungle quickly . . . chased out. The survivors were good men, mostly, the captain having picked the best of the lot for the trip. Phelan and Jackson had returned, and a handful of others. All of them were filthy, their clothes torn and dirty, their eyes haunted.

The last man to climb aboard was William Wrickitts, and he nearly didn't make it. He was moving clumsily, like a stunned bumblebee bumping against a windowpane. Attempting to swing his leg over the side of the boat, he clipped his foot on the edge and lost his balance. He reached out for the shoulder of the man in front of him, trying to keep from falling, but his hands failed to grab hold.

He lurched backward and seemed headed for the sea, but the strong hand of the captain grabbed a fistful of Wrickitts's shirt and hauled him upright. "Get this man some help," he barked. "He is not well."

Manny began to count the missing. The ship's doctor was gone, and the strange scientist who'd traveled with them was gone too. Manny risked a quick glimpse at the man's ship-bound assistant. The boy's expression was one of stunned disbelief.

Manny looked away and continued the grim count. The first mate, a good sailor and a decent man, gone. Three more good sailors gone as well. Six lost in all, the party sliced in two.

"But, Captain," began a sailor named Duffy, "where are the others?"

Duffy was a competent and well-liked seaman, but he was known to be more than a little simpleminded. Jaw clenched, Captain Eagling glared at him but then seemed to remember Duffy's limitations. "The jungle took them," he said, shaking his head. "The jungle took them all."

The words echoed like thunder across the suddenly silent deck. A moment later, the captain broke the spell he'd cast. "You, Boy Obed!" he called, spotting a ship's boy named Obed Macy. "Secure this trunk deep in the hold."

A small leather-bound trunk was plucked from the launch and handed to the silent child. Obed was a reclusive boy, small for his age, but strong for his size. The combination doomed him to the grim job of hold rat. As a result, he spent as much time down in the dark, stinking confines of the hold as Manny spent aloft, nestled in the blue skies of the rigging.

Manny slid over a few steps to stand beside Mario, the two touching shoulders lightly. The others called them "the Spanish brothers," and it was not a term of endearment. They were young, foreign, and orphaned, with only their skills and each other to their name. They were dressed much as the rest of the crew, with loose shirts, pants salvaged from strips of sailcloth, and battered black sun-shielding hats worn on the back of their heads. But unlike the others, the Spanish brothers also wore headscarves and thick undershirts, both tightly bound in what they assured the others was "the Spanish style." Their olive Iberian complexions had darkened further under the relentless sun.

The botanist's stunned assistant, new to the sea and his own skin still red and peeling, seemed to wake to the real world just long enough to recognize the trunk. "The doctor's specimen case," he mumbled, brushing his fingers across it as it passed.

"Yes," said the captain, the anger draining from his voice. "The jungle took much from us, but we took something back."

Obed Macy carried the precious cargo to the hold, disappearing down the aft hatch into the darkness below.

It was a darkness from which neither he nor the *Polaris* would ever truly emerge.

CHAPTER 1

LOCKED IN

Owen had just helped to round up his fellow ship's boys and bring them to the captain's cabin. For his trouble, Captain Eagling shoved him in last. Unprepared for the sharp cuff to the shoulder, Owen stumbled into the low square room, nearly bumping his head on the oil lamp suspended from the ceiling.

"Stay in there until I come get you," called the captain. "This meeting is no place for children—and we've already lost one of you lot."

Owen straightened up quickly, brushing off his vest and hoping none of the others had seen him stumble. A name shot through his mind like a winter chill—Obed Macy, the boy they'd lost—but he had no time for such thoughts now. "All right, I'll keep an eye on them for you," he called back.

Captain Eagling responded by slamming the door. Owen had half expected that. What he hadn't expected was the sound of iron sliding into place.

"What was that?" asked Henry. There was a soft, hesitant quality to his voice that annoyed Owen.

"We're locked in," he snapped.

In the glow of the small lamp, the cabin was only a little brighter than the drizzly gray twilight outside. Owen had been in the captain's cabin countless times—he was, after all, the cabin boy. The botanist's assistant had been in a few times too, back when his master was still around to justify his shipboard existence. But for the other four ship's boys this was a new experience. Owen watched with a certain pride as their eyes drank in the little luxuries, so unlike their own cramped quarters: teacups in the snug little cupboard, ornate maps on the wall.

Mario nodded toward a knife and fork on the table and spoke in a soft Spanish accent, "Think those are real silver?"

Owen eyed him suspiciously. Mario was standing next to his brother, as always. Both were lean and vaguely birdlike, but he knew they were hard workers and that Manny, in particular, was an acrobat aloft. "Of course they're silver—and they've been counted!" he warned.

Mario put his hands up, palms out to show that they were empty.

"Is there anything else we ain't allowed to touch?" asked Aaron Burnett.

He was a powder monkey, responsible for carrying gunpowder to the ship's cannons. The *Polaris* had four of them, not too bad for an armed merchantman. Hauling gunpowder in the heat of battle was dangerous work, and Aaron had been on deck when a powder monkey named Josué had blown up trying to carry two cartridges at once. Rumor had it that bits of the boy could still be found up in the topsails. Aaron had become exceedingly cautious ever since. He measured his steps and the gunpowder with equal care. Owen didn't bother to answer him. He knew that the timid boy would be no trouble.

But there was one boy who might be. Owen's eyes landed on the only ship's boy left to consider: the new hold rat now that Obed Macy had gone missing. Owen sensed him more than saw him, skulking silently in the far corner of the cabin, hiding his scarred face in the shadows. Thacher Maybin . . .

Shouting out on the deck interrupted Owen's thoughts. As he rushed over to press his ear against the locked door, the reason for their confinement came back to him. An all-hands meeting had been called, and the ship's boys were not welcome. At the very least, there would be swearing. At the worst . . . He didn't want to think about that.

A light rain was falling and the seas were up. A storm was approaching, but the tensions on board had little to do with the worsening weather. The uneasy feeling had been rising steadily for the last week, ever since the doomed inland expedition had returned and the ship had immediately set sail for home.

The loss of so many men had taken a toll. Everyone on board had lost a friend or six, and of course, their absence left that much more work for the survivors. The demise of the popular and proficient first mate was an especially heavy blow. Now the former second mate, the dour and hard-driving William Shannahan, oversaw the day-to-day running of the ship.

And almost as bad for the crew's morale as the loss of their comrades was the lack of any real explanation. What exactly had happened out there in the dark precincts of the jungle? The captain had forbidden any open discussion of the matter. To question the captain was to risk flogging, or even hanging. But down in the crew quarters, Owen had heard the whispered rumors spread.

There was talk of a strange tropical sickness and wild tales of a beast in the night. And as much as he'd heard, Owen knew there was much more being shared in secret. The sailors had never trusted the captain's nephew. But trusted or not, he'd witnessed some of the strange happenings below deck himself. The sights and sounds—and even the smells—seemed to bring those rumors to life.

Now the ship had dropped anchor, sheltering from the wind in the lee of a small island, preparing to ride out the storm, in every sense. With the dark mood nearly unbearable, a meeting had finally been called.

Suddenly, there were more shouts on deck. Owen leaned in, but the wooden door was too thick—and the wind outside too strong—for him to make out the words. He cupped his hand around his right ear and moved over to the narrow gap of the doorframe. He could sense the others crowding around behind him.

"What're they saying?" asked Aaron.

"SHHHH!" said Owen, closing his eyes and trying to concentrate. The steady drone of half a dozen people talking at once was mostly drowned out by the wind. But as the gusts died down for a moment, a single shout cut through the air.

"Hand over Wrickitts!"

Owen heard it clearly, not just the words but the voice. It was the new first mate, William Shannahan. But who was he shouting at? It couldn't possibly be—

"Stand down, Shannahan."

Owen gasped. It was the captain's voice. "He's a sick man and he'll get our care," the captain continued. There was a murmuring of agreement.

"Sick?" shouted Shannahan as the murmuring changed to an angry grumbling. "The man is in—"

The whipping wind returned, whistling through the gap in the doorframe and carrying away the rest of Shannahan's words. Owen slumped to the floor, stunned by what he'd just heard. The first mate arguing with the captain . . .

"What did you hear?" repeated Aaron.

Owen looked up at him, his eyes wide with disbelief, and spoke a single word. It was a word that even sailors, who called sharks "Johnnies" and made light of the most dangerous conditions, seldom dared to speak. It was a word like dark magic.

"Mutiny."

CHAPTER 2

A SOUND LIKE THUNDER

"Here, try this," said Henry.

Owen raised his eyes from the floor. "Put that back in the case!" he said. "It's fragile. Not even the captain drinks from it."

Henry turned the ornate little glass over in his hands, examining its etched surface. Owen was sure he'd drop it. "It's decorative!" Owen said, deploying his most formidable vocabulary word.

"But it's made of glass," countered Henry.

"That's why it's decorative!" said Owen. "And if you break it, he'll hang you with the first mate." Owen gave up and turned back to the door. He had bigger worries. He pressed his ear against the doorframe again, but all he heard was whipping wind and muffled shouts. He listened harder, but now all he heard was the botanist's assistant, still talking and filling up his other ear. He turned back to him, exasperated. "Be quiet! We need to find out what's happening."

Once again, Henry held the glass out to him. "This will help," he said. "Glass is an excellent conductor of sound."

Owen squinted up at him. He didn't like this boy much, and just watching him hold the glass made Owen nervous—but he was desperate. "Show me how," he said.

Henry knelt down next to him. "You put the open end on the door," he said, "and then you put your ear on the closed end."

Owen took hold of the glass carefully and followed the instructions. The others all leaned in, trying to measure his reaction. "Anything?" said Manny.

"Shhhh!" Owen hissed, his ear pressed against the glass. "I hear them . . ."

His voice trailed off as the argument started up again. The glass amplified the words and spared him the whistling wind in the door gap.

"There he is!" called a voice Owen couldn't quite place.

"It's Wrickitts—dear Lord, look at him!" Owen tried to understand what was happening. Had William Wrickitts heard his name called and dragged himself out of his sick berth? A louder shout interrupted his thoughts: "Get him!"

The words were followed by more shouts and heavy thumping sounds. The argument had become a scuffle. But why argue over a man who could barely walk? A man who could no longer even speak?

Owen tried to picture Wrickitts, remembering how he'd

barely cleared the ship's rail on his return from the jungle, and how the odd hitch in his walk had gotten worse and worse in the days since. He'd shambled around, dragging his feet heavily across the deck, clumsier and more confused with each passing day. A strange and gruesome rash had broken out on his skin, and he'd fallen mute, either with nothing to say or no way to say it. That was when he'd been confined to a sickbed to recuperate—or at least to prevent his devilish ailment from spreading. Rumor had it he'd even taken to perfuming himself to cover the heavy smell of his decay.

Owen hadn't given it much thought, except to pity the man, formerly one of their best and strongest sailors. Imagine an old salt like Wrickitts reduced to perfuming himself, using a gift procured for a lady, perhaps, on his own leathery hide. But now something else occurred to Owen: the rumors of the "strange tropical illness" that had cut a deadly swath through the landing party, and the reality of the one laying poor Wrickitts low . . . Was that why the mutineers wanted him? His illness? But to what end?

The answer came quickly. "We've got him, Mr. Shannahan!"

"Do as you must!" called the first mate.

"Don't you touch that man!" called the captain. "He is under our care, and if we must fly the quarantine flag in port, then so be—"

A sound like thunder cut off the captain's words. No glass was needed to hear it through the door. Owen flinched as the amplified blast rang in his ear. The others in the cabin jumped back, and one or two even shouted with alarm. Owen leaned back in. He held his breath and listened harder than he ever had in his life. Approaching storm or not, he knew that was no clap of thunder.

It was a gunshot.

"Throw him over the side!" called Shannahan. Between the wind and waves, Owen could only imagine the next sound: a soft and silky splash he knew all too well. He'd heard it several times before—during burials at sea.

"My Lord," he whispered.

"You mutinous cur!" called the captain. Owen was relieved to hear his voice, if not his words. "I'll sail into New York with the lot of you hanging from the yardarms!"

The shouts intensified, and the scuffling gained such strength that Owen could feel it through the wood of the deck beneath him. He sprang to his feet and tossed the precious glass back over his shoulder. He didn't need it anymore. The time for words was over. It was open mutiny now.

Three shots rang out in quick succession—the officers' pistols. Shrieks of pain mixed with the shouts of rage, telling Owen that the rest of the work would be done with blades and hands.

He rammed his shoulder hard into the heavy door, only to bounce off. "Help me!" he called. "We must break it down."

He turned back to the others, but they had taken cover as soon as they'd heard the gunshots. Aaron and Thacher were huddled under the table, and the Spanish brothers were kneeling along the wall. Only Henry was still standing close by, staring down at the broken glass at his feet in what seemed to Owen a spell of stupid consternation.

Owen glared back at him, the other boy's slender frame silhouetted against the heavy glass windows at the back of the cabin. Outside, night was falling and the seas were rising. The waves tossed angrily under the fading light, their foamy tops an ashen gray, and the vessel dipped and pitched and rolled under their command.

Out on deck, the fight was already ending. There was one last scream, one last sailor succumbing to some unseen slash or phantom stab.

Owen turned slowly back toward the door. He desperately hoped that the next sound he heard would be Captain Eagling, bloodied but triumphant, opening the door and releasing the young crew members he had kept safe.

But as the moment stretched agonizingly on, the only sounds were those of wind and waves. And when a human voice rose at last, it was the last one Owen wanted to hear.

Shannahan.

"Over the side with 'em, boys!" he called. The silky splashes rose once more in Owen's mind—bodies committed to the deep with neither goodwill nor prayer. There was a brief pause as the mutineers did their dirty work and then: "Him too. And let it be done."

No name was given for the last body tossed over the rail, and none was needed.

The captain, thought Owen. *My captain.*

CHAPTER 3

TRIAL BY FIRE

Aaron lifted his head and drew in a long breath through his nose. "Is that smoke?" he said.

Owen sniffed the air. It was smoke. He leaned closer to the door. A gust of wind whistled through the gap, and suddenly the smell was stronger. "We have to get out of here!" he said.

This time, the others didn't argue. They rushed the door together. Owen and Aaron, the two largest, were in front. They buried their shoulders into the wood as the smaller boys pushed from behind. But the wood was thick. Owen's shoulder ached as they drew back and crashed into the door for the third, fourth, and then fifth time. Stars burst and swirled across his vision. Finally, on the sixth try, he heard a dry, splintering sound. The door was pulling away from one of its heavy iron hinges. He shifted over, targeting that edge, and with two more bull rushes, the old door broke free.

Owen stepped through first, squinting into flickering firelight and coughing on thick smoke. His fists were clenched, ready for a fight, but the threat he saw was far more explosive. "What the blazes?" he said as the others filed out behind him.

It was a fitting oath, because in the center of the deck, a fire was burning. A length of rolled-up sailcloth had been curled into a semicircle, with one end aflame and the other end wedged beneath a wooden barrel.

"That's gunpowder!" shouted Aaron.

The fire had already rounded the bend in the cloth and was creeping forward despite the light rain, the heat drying the cloth as the flames marched onward with an ominous sizzle. If those flames reached the barrel, Owen knew that it would explode with enough force and fire to ignite all the gunpowder below deck too.

"Get the buckets from the pump!" shouted Owen.

"There's no time for that," called Aaron. Owen didn't doubt him—the powder monkey knew more about the treacherous nature of combustion than the others ever would.

Owen rushed across the rolling deck. He could feel the warmth of the flames against his skin as he leapt over the center of the burning cloth to reach the barrel. His heart pounded as he crouched down low and wheeled the little cask off the rolled cloth. Aaron rushed up next to him and kicked the end of the cloth across the deck, just to be sure.

Owen nodded his approval and then headed over to the seawater pump to get the first bucket of water himself. He cleared the steps to the low forecastle in a single leap. It wasn't quite night yet, but the heavy clouds made it seem darker than the hour as they doused the burning cloth.

With the immediate disaster averted, Owen finally had time to wonder: Where in all this gray gloom were the mutineers? And why on earth or sea would they try to blow up the ship?

As he turned to haul his empty bucket back where he'd found it, he got his answer. A flash of far-off lightning lit the turbulent sea, and he saw a long boat crest a longer wave.

"Look!" he shouted as Aaron and Manny walked past with buckets of their own.

"Where?" Manny called over the low rumble of thunder just now reaching the ship.

Owen waited for it to subside. "To leeward, two points off the beam."

The others peered out over the rail waiting for the next lightning strike. The ship's launch appeared again, half full of men and making for the small island the ship had been sheltering behind. Owen took in as much as he could in the quick flicker of light. "They've set up a sailing rig," he said, eyeing the little mast in the middle of the boat and the tightly furled cloth wrapped around it. He was sure they'd taken the spare navigation equipment as well: a quadrant, a compass or two, and probably a Bowditch as well. Captain Eagling had sworn that nothing aboard was as valuable as Nathaniel Bowditch's encyclopedia of navigation, and Owen knew he never set sail without a spare copy. "They'll shelter upon the island tonight and then set sail in the morning."

"Aye, but . . . why?" said Aaron, his voice betraying his bafflement.

That is the question, thought Owen, staring into the storm. *Why capture a ship only to abandon it in an angry sea? And why shut off all hope of return by blowing the ship up behind you?* Even in the deepening gloom, he could see that the launch was riding low in the water, weighed down with men and supplies. And as hard as those men were rowing, they were still a long, hard pull from a small and unknown shore.

He had one final thought as he turned away, darker than the onrushing storm: *I hope none of them make it.*

CHAPTER 4

ALONE ON THE WAVES

Two events occurred in quick succession, and Henry—taking an analytical approach, as usual—deemed them both regrettable.

First, night fell. Under the heavy blanket of clouds, the sky became a pure black.

Then, as if waiting only for the cover of darkness, the storm hit. No longer far off, the thunder and lightning were now simultaneous, loud enough to stun and bright enough to blind.

The rain fell in lukewarm sheets as the ship's boys scrambled across the dark and treacherous deck, taking in the last of the sails and battening down the hatches to keep the water out. Henry heard their shouts and grunts over the whipping wind, but he himself had no idea where to go or what to do. He was in the waist of the ship, the low stretch between the raised fore-castle in the front and the quarterdeck aft. Soaked to the bone and blind as a bat, he had never felt so exposed or helpless in his life. It was all he could do to keep his balance, and as the waves rose higher, even that became too much. The *Polaris* lurched abruptly to the side, and Henry slid helplessly down the rain-slick deck. His soggy, treadless boots provided no traction whatsoever as he hurtled toward a roiling sea that he could only hear. *This is how I die*, he thought, panic and resignation mixing like the fresh rainwater falling into the salty waves.

"Ooooof!" he gasped. The sharp pain in his ribs told him that he was still alive—at least for now. He reached down and grabbed for whatever he'd just crashed into. His desperate, clutching hands told him it was the ship's rail that had saved his life. Lightning lit the sky again, and he gazed down into the frothy tumult below. It seemed mere feet away, but suddenly the distance began to grow. As the wave passed beneath the ship, the low side rose up. Henry soon found himself clutching the rail for dear life, not to avoid falling forward but to avoid flying backward across the deck and tumbling over the other side.

He cast his eyes around desperately and saw the door to the captain's cabin crack open, the faint light of the hanging lamp still burning within. A shadow slipped inside and the gap closed. The others were already retreating inside. He unwrapped one sore arm from the rail and took a wobbly half step toward the cabin. As he did, the ship rolled once again, dipping him back down toward the sea. He threw himself against the rail.

He felt the ocean spray against his cheek and tasted its salt on his lips. Slowly—very slowly—he began inching his way along the rail toward the cabin. Though he was no sailor, Henry was skilled at observing natural phenomena. Even in the dark, he quickly realized that the rolling swells arrived at more or less regular intervals. He timed his movements accordingly, clinging tight when the waves lifted him high in the air and moving forward quickly as the ship briefly leveled off. And it was in one of those precious moments—when gravity was restored and the deck was less perilous—that he dashed across the quarterdeck for the cabin door.

He grabbed the handle as the boat began to pitch deeply, but he remembered too late that the door had been knocked from its hinges. It was held in place only by its iron lock. As the ship rose higher and higher on its side, Henry clung tightly to the door handle. Under his weight, he felt the soggy wood around that lock begin to splinter and crack.

Oh no, oh no, oh no!

Letting go meant flying straight into the waves. Holding on meant doing the same a few seconds later—with a door on top of him.

Suddenly, an arm appeared in the dim gap between the broken hinges. Its strong hand grabbed on tight to Henry's shoulder. Once the boat settled and began to roll back, the hand tugged him toward the gap. As the boat passed through level, Henry turned sideways and scrambled inside.

And there, in the lamplight, he saw the face of the last person he'd expected. Henry mumbled a quick "thank you," but Owen ignored him. The strong-armed cabin boy was already at work lifting the door back onto one broken hinge and sliding some slim piece of metal—a fork, perhaps—through to keep it there.

Henry clutched the other side of the doorframe as the boat began to roll again. The hanging lamp stretched the shadows as it swung. He saw five other sodden boys. Including himself, their ages couldn't total more than eighty years. And yet, as the thunder roared overhead, he realized that this was it. All that was left. They were utterly on their own.

"Will we survive this storm?" he said as the thunder faded.

For a few moments, no one answered. The only sounds were the wind and sea outside and the teacups tinkling in their snug cupboard.

"Better men than us have already died tonight," said Owen. His words were angry, but his voice was sad. "But yes, we're anchored firmly in five fathoms, and the island will take the worst of the wind. It will be a dirty night, and we'll have plenty of pumping to do, but we'll make it."

Henry nodded, still clutching the doorframe tightly as Owen moved easily across the rolling floor of the little cabin in a bent-kneed crouch. Henry looked down at the bare feet of the others and then at his own soggy boots. Owen wheeled around to look at him. "But you have a lot to learn," he said, "if you hope to last another day."

CHAPTER 5

GHOST STORIES

They rode out the storm in the captain's cabin. Most of the crew had been at sea for long enough that seasickness was a distant though unpleasant memory, but not everyone was so lucky. Henry threw up into a chamber pot and then stared balefully down at what he'd done. His seasickness actually seemed to get worse as the rolling swells began to subside. Manny recalled those miserable days, when a gentle rocking could be as bad as a raucous rolling.

Soon the wind began to die down too, the steady howling reduced to an occasional loud gust. Manny watched the swinging lamp and saw the storm fade in the settling of its shadows.

"Just a squall after all," said Aaron.

"No," said Owen softly. "The seas were too high. It was a storm, all right. We caught the tail end of it." His voice sounded distracted and distant, so different from its usual bluster that Manny turned around to look at him. He was sitting in the captain's chair, contemplating a teacup. That was the captain's too, Manny figured. Owen was visibly devastated, like a puppy that had lost its master. An arrogant know-it-all puppy, but still.

One by one, the survivors rose to their feet, except for Owen. The captain's cabin, while a little low for actual adults, was the perfect height for ship's boys. And whether they'd ridden out a storm or a squall inside, it had lasted only a few hours. Now it was time to see to the ship and salvage what sleep they could from the remainder of the night.

Manny knew one thing for sure: They'd all need their rest. The next day would dawn on a boat without captain, carpenter, gunner, or doctor. Every crew member rated able seaman had been lost to the sea—by choice, by blade, or by bullet. Names and faces flashed through Manny's mind. Maybe not friends, exactly—they were too unequal for that—but some of them had been kind and generous. If there was one silver lining to all that rain, Manny thought with a shudder, it was that there'd be none of their blood left on the deck.

"I suppose we should head below deck to sleep, then," said Aaron tentatively.

Manny shuddered again. The cramped confines below deck were dark and dank on any sailing ship, but lately on the *Polaris* they had become something even worse. And Manny wasn't the only one to feel it. No one moved for a few long moments. Finally, Thacher broke the silence.

"Should we?" he said, his voice little more than a whisper.

Manny was shocked. It was a crazy thing to say. The crew always slept below deck—on this ship, on every ship. And yet . . . After what had happened on this vessel just hours earlier, and with only the six of them left aboard, could anything else on the *Polaris* truly be called crazy?

Reflexively, a few heads looked back at Owen, but he seemed unaware of the exchange. He was lost in thought, still sitting there contemplating his teacup. *Has he found a crack?* wondered Manny. *Or has he cracked himself? And if so, is he the only one?* There'd been sniffles from some of the others as the storm died down, and a few little sobs they'd tried to time with the fading thunder. With raw survival no longer at stake, Manny knew, the dire situation was starting to hit home.

With no one challenging him, Thacher continued, his voice a little louder. "Should we head below? Now, after all that has happened? Now, on this pitch-black night? Now, when we would be all alone down there?"

The questions hung in the air like stars.

"I don't want to," admitted Aaron.

"I hate it down there," added Henry. Manny looked at him. He was such a strange boy. He seemed to live in his head and had barely been seen or heard since the loss of his own master.

"I do too." This time the voice came from right beside Manny. It was Mario. Manny flashed a quick warning look. *Don't forget*, it said. There was no need for more. Mario knew the reason well: The darkness below might hide dangers, but it hid secrets too.

Mario shrugged and added, "There is something bad down there. And now, with no men left . . ."

With Owen still locked in silence, all eyes turned to Manny, who let out a long sigh and then an admission. "There *is* something bad down there. Something . . . wrong."

"Something," said Thacher, "or someone."

Aaron gasped, and Manny barely managed to avoid doing the same. Once again, Thacher had dared to speak the unspeakable. And in doing so, he had broken down a dam. The stories began to flow forth. And they weren't normal stories.

They were ghost stories.

"I've seen things," whispered Aaron.

The room went silent. Manny stared back at Aaron. Even Owen glanced up from his cup.

"What have you seen?" coaxed Thacher, the pale scar above his left eyebrow glowing softly in the lamplight, giving him an expression both curious and strange.

"Well . . ." Aaron began. Manny leaned in a little closer. "It's shadows, mostly. It's hard to say; it's always so dark down there."

Manny pictured the world below deck. There were no windows at all. During the day, light filtered in through any open grates or hatches on deck. But at night or in foul weather, there was barely any light. A lamp hanging fore and aft and maybe a trickle of moonlight, at most. There might be other lamps burning in the officers' berths or the carpenter's cabin, but precious little good that did the crew.

Aaron went on. "So when I say shadows, it could be just a shadow of a shadow under a full moon, but the thing is—"

Thacher cut in: "The shadow doesn't look right." Everyone turned to look at him. "It doesn't move right."

"Yes!" Aaron agreed. "That's it exactly. It looks human enough, when the light catches it. But the way it moves—shuffles along. At first, well, I thought it was poor old Wrickitts, but then he took to his sickbed."

This time it was Mario cutting in: "And the shadow haunted us all the more." Manny shot another warning look over, but Mario ignored it. "I saw it too. Always late at night, always out of the clew of my eye, along the wall, at the door, never out in the open."

"And then there's the sound," added Aaron. "A horrible sound, a—a—" He searched for the word and then found it. "A dragging."

"A dry, raw scraping," added Thacher.

Manny eyed him carefully. Thacher was throwing fuel on the fire. What was he up to? The story below deck was that Thacher had come from a respected Boston family that had been ruined—a rich family turned poor. His fine education was cut short, and being the youngest of the brothers, he was sold into servitude to help pay off the family's debts. *Is it true?* Manny wondered. Thacher definitely talked the part—but he didn't get those scars at a piano lesson.

"Shadows, sounds," said Owen, finally putting down his cup and looking up. "That could have been anything. The ship is full of sights and sounds at night. A crew mate on the way back from the head, rats in the scuppers . . ."

Owen's words trailed off. He looked small sitting in the big chair. Thacher looked down at him and a slow smile spread across his face. His other scar, the one on his cheek, folded over on itself like a white worm writhing. "Aye, no doubt, so many sights and sounds. But then, of course, there is the smell . . ."

Owen looked away, and that's when Manny knew he'd seen something too—seen it and heard it and smelled it. Thacher went on, choosing his words with care: "A smell like rotting flowers, at their sweetest just before they turn brown and fall away . . ."

"That was the worst part," said Aaron. "The shadow would shuffle across some dark corner, scraping its way by like fingernails on stone, and then, when you were lying there, telling yourself it was just your imagination—"

"Or a dream," added Mario.

Aaron nodded. "Just then, you'd smell it."

"The dense funk of the crew and all their earthly odors turned into a field of dying flowers," said Thacher.

The cabin was silent for a moment.

"Not like a flower," said Henry. It had been so long since he'd spoken that Manny had almost forgotten he was there. But all eyes were on him now. He shifted uncomfortably at the attention.

"What did you say?" said Thacher, a hint of warning in his voice.

"It's just that I am a botanist's assistant—well, I was—and I have smelled something like that before. It's sweet, as you say, but more like a fungus. Well, certain funguses . . ."

He descended into mumbling: "Sickly sweet, to be sure . . . but a certain yeastiness to it . . . quite unmistakable once—"

Thacher abruptly cut him off. "I'll tell you what it is," he spat.

Don't say it, don't say it, don't say it, thought Manny.

"It's Obed Macy!"

Manny's blood went cold. He'd said it.

"Thing is, Obed liked flowers," said Thacher. "At least, before he took that chest down into the hold and disappeared for good."

"What do you mean?" said Aaron.

"I was with him when he came back from shore once. I'd spent my money on sweets, but all he got for his was a sad bunch of cut flowers. 'What are those for?' I asked him, and do you know what he said?"

Thacher looked around the room.

"What?" breathed Mario.

"'Fer me pillow,'" said Thacher, imitating Obed's voice and accent perfectly. "'So me dark little world don't smell so bad.'"

More silence.

"That's right!" crowed Thacher. "It's a hard life being a hold rat. You think the smells are bad where you lay your heads, try working in the hold, walking over all that stinking sloshing bilge water. You're more liable to step upon a drowned rat than dry wood."

Thacher glared around the room, daring anyone to challenge his claims. "I'm the hold rat now, but I'll tell you something funny—something most peculiar . . ."

He paused, and Manny knew for certain that what he would say next would not be funny at all. "I've been all through that hold looking for his body. Haven't found a thing . . . but it smells awfully sweet down there these days."

"It's him . . ." said Aaron. "Obed Macy."

Thacher nodded solemnly, but then another thought occurred to Aaron. "Or it could be old Wrickitts and his perfume."

Thacher cocked his head, considering this new possibility. Manny groaned softly.

It was all over. Two potential ghosts were simply too many for the young crew. By a vote of five to two the decision was made: The survivors would sleep above deck until they reached port or sank the ship trying.

"Of course you two are welcome to sleep down there," Thacher said to the no voters, Owen and Manny.

Owen let out a dismissive snort and said, "Like I'd trust you urchins alone in the captain's cabin. The silver in here belongs to my family, you know."

Whether Owen meant it or not, Thacher flinched when he heard those words. So his family had sold him off, after all, thought Manny, along with the silverware, no doubt.

Manny shot Mario another look. It was less of a warning this time—Mario's yes vote had already been cast—and more of a plea: *I hope you know what you're doing.* Sharing this little cabin might feel safer, and even cozy, to the others, but it was a little too close for comfort for them.

Reluctantly, Owen unhinged the broken door and the young crew shuffled out into the night. The rain had stopped, and the dark clouds had begun to pull apart. A hint of moonlight shined down on the deck as the ship rocked gently to and fro. Owen and Aaron removed first the long wooden battens and then the thick tarpaulin cover from the aft hatch with sure, practiced hands. As they waited to head below and retrieve their meager possessions, the others took deep breaths of fresh salt air. All of them hoped it would be the sweetest thing they'd smell that night.

CHAPTER 6

A WORLD DARK AND DANK

This is a mistake, thought Owen.

Even worse, it was a mistake that he'd allowed the others to force on him. But then, it always seemed to be that way. Had he ever been wrong about such a thing on his own? About anything, really? He considered it. *No*, he decided. *Not me.*

He stepped aside and let the others head down the hatch. This hadn't been his idea, so why should he go first? The ladder was sturdy and angled—almost like stairs, really—and he chastised himself as he headed down. He'd been lost in his own head back in the cabin—moping over his uncle, turning over that stupid cup—and now it was too late. It just wasn't proper for anyone to sleep above deck. He corrected himself: anyone but the captain. The captain . . . He'd been his mentor, his kin, and every once in a while, maybe even his friend. But now he was gone.

Owen felt himself slipping back into something far darker and deeper than the shadowy space below deck, but he shook it off. He couldn't afford any more self-pity. He descended the ladder, last in line. As he sank below the hatch, even the faint light of half a moon vanished. He was halfway down before Mario found the aft lamp and lit it.

Owen reached the bottom. Water had slipped in through the hatches and grates, and he felt the slick wet wood under his feet. The *Polaris* was a sturdy ship, but she'd never been the tightest or the driest.

The heavy old lamp seemed to create more shadows than light, and Owen eyed the edges of that light, where the shadows gave way to pure black in the corners and farther on. And then, despite himself, he pulled a deep whiff of air into his nostrils.

The smell that greeted him was a dank mix, with hints of human sweat and the mold growing in the dark. It wasn't what anyone would call pleasant, but it was as it should be down here. Owen let the breath out through his lips.

"Let's take the lamp with us," said Aaron.

Owen felt like he should object, assert himself. He'd been outnumbered on the original decision, brushed aside due to his distraction. But now he'd recovered, and taking the lamp was another breach of protocol. Owen opened his mouth, but nothing came out. He looked up at the grates. On a clear night, with the moon and stars above, they let in almost enough light for a dark-adapted eye to see by. But the grates were still covered for the storm and pitch-black.

"Yes, let's take it," said Mario, and the next thing Owen knew, Aaron had taken it down.

Owen remained silent. *Outvoted again*, he told himself. But there was something else going on, something apart from weak light and deep shadows and what he did or did not smell. He was standing just below the aft hatch and facing forward. He still hadn't taken a look behind him. Because that was where the officers' berths were.

And the officers were all dead, or worse: traitors. He remembered the sight of the launch heading out into the rising seas. Dead *and* traitors.

And suddenly the light was on the move, heading away from him. Owen hustled to catch up. The group stayed tightly packed as they passed by bulkheads and beams. With too many bodies in between him and the lamp, Owen could barely see a thing, but he knew from memory that they were passing the breadroom.

"Should we?" ventured Mario.

"No!" Owen barked. There'd be no midnight snacks while he was around. What was this, anarchy? It felt good to assert himself, at last. He shouldered his way closer to the front of the group as they arrived at the crew's berth.

He looked around at a museum of the dead. Battered trunks against the walls, coats and hats hanging from pegs, foul-weather boots flopping over on themselves . . . Everywhere he looked, he saw the scattered possessions of dead sailors. He'd seen such ownerless debris before: when the expedition had returned, cut in half. But all signs of those lost men had been pushed aside by the remaining sailors, quickly snatched up or displaced by the hustle and bustle of a working ship. This time, there'd be no recovering. The wounds were too deep. Owen felt a shiver rise from his core. "Gather your things, boys," he called. "And make it quick."

The group scattered to the edges of the berth, to the odd corners and slivers of space where they'd been exiled by the big, burly, and as often as not foulmouthed sailors. The *Polaris* not being the driest of ships, nearly all the sailors had opted for hammocks rather than thin mattresses. For the ship's boys, there was no choice. They gathered their hammocks quickly. Some of them shouldered their small sea trunks and others just pawed through theirs for dry clothes or good-luck charms.

Owen's trunk was too large to carry easily, and he figured he could always come back for whatever he needed. He removed some essentials and then pulled his small silver cross and whalebone comb from their hiding place in the trunk's lining and pocketed them both. As he slammed the trunk closed, a large wave passed under the ship—one last reminder of the storm. He wobbled on his feet. He heard the putrid bilge water slosh and slop in the hold below and prepared himself for the wave of foul odor that usually followed. But the scent that reached his nose this time smelled more of—

"Flowers," said Thacher.

Henry said something in response, but it was drowned out by the sound of trunks slamming shut.

"Let's go!" said three of them at once.

A moment later, the lamplight was heading back the way they'd come, the darkness shrinking before it and growing after it. Owen took one more look back as they retreated. What he saw was a dark and dank world. It had been so very familiar once, but now it seemed exceedingly strange. Death seemed to permeate the old ship right down to its beams.

And then he saw something else. At the edge of the light, at the edge of his vision: a shadow. And true, it was but one shadow among many, but this one wasn't deepening back into darkness.

This one was moving. This one was following.

A night filled with bloodshed and ghost stories was edging toward dawn now, but not all the dead, it seemed, were content to rest.

And Owen, who'd been the last one down the hatch, was the first one to climb back up.

CHAPTER 7

THE FIRST STEP

Since he could walk, or at least since he could swim, it had been Owen's dream to one day occupy the captain's cabin on a ship such as the *Polaris*.

But not like this.

Comfort was not the issue. As the ship rocked gently beneath him, his hanging hammock cradled him softly and stayed more or less level. No, it was the tragic circumstances that bothered him. That, and the company.

The others were arrayed all around him, anywhere they could hook two ends of a hammock. Every available sleeping space was taken, with the notable exception of the captain's bed. It was a sturdy wooden shelf built into the wall and topped with a feather pillow and a soft red blanket. As comfortable as it looked, the thought of anyone else sleeping there seemed ludicrous. The once-stately cabin itself now felt more like a one-room schoolhouse. It was all so out of order that it boggled the cabin boy's mind.

It wouldn't have been so bad if we'd set the watches, he thought. *Then half of us would be on deck.* But safely at anchor and exhausted, they'd called off the watches. It was a collective decision, made simply by not doing it. It troubled him, but he was so tired, and it was true enough: There were no mates left to lead the watches anyway. They'd figure it all out in the morning, he hoped.

He rolled over, scrunched his eyes closed, and tried again to sleep. The *Polaris* did its part, gently rocking back and forth. But it was no use.

Owen lay awake for most of the night. On the few occasions he managed to nod off, he dreamed of bloody mutiny. He'd wake, confusing it for memory until he recalled that he couldn't possibly have seen any of it from inside the cabin. Then he'd remember the utter helplessness he'd felt, locked in as the fighting erupted, vainly ramming his shoulder against the thick door. Then came the tragic end, and the sight of the traitors cresting a wave in the launch, disappearing into darkness. Curse them.

All around him, the others fought their own nocturnal battles. He heard Manny talking in his sleep a few feet away, mumbling something in Spanish before punching a half-formed fist at the air. Striking out at a nightmare, Manny nearly hit Mario.

In a darker corner by the door, Aaron sniffled. Or was it the botanist's assistant? It was too dark to tell, and Owen was honestly glad. Whoever was crying, they deserved at least that little bit of privacy.

It was the first peaceful thought he'd had all night, and moments later, he finally fell into a sound sleep. He woke just before dawn. He shifted in his hammock and craned his neck over its canvas edge. He stared out the bank of windows at the back of the cabin until he saw it. *There*, he thought as the first streaks of gray rose like vapor from the eastern horizon.

He loved this moment, how the sunrise brightened the ocean below faster than it lit the sky above. Faint light spread across the face of the sea, hinting at its vast depths and all the living things moving there, from the littlest minnow to the mightiest whale. He gave up on sleep and tried to think of nothing but what was happening beyond those windows.

A thin slice of clear light spread across the horizon, and the sky turned a brighter gray above it, like lead melting upward. The sea lit up with the first subtle shades of green and blue. And then, like a big egg or a small miracle, the first golden rays of the sun cracked the horizon. Owen knew now that the day ahead would be sunny and fair, and he allowed himself a small smile.

But a moment later, the memories came crashing back. The smile fell from his face, and his jaw locked in firm resolve. He looked around the cabin in the dim light. Drool ran down Henry's cheek; Aaron rolled onto his side, away from the light; and Thacher lay so still that he might just as easily have been dead.

With no one on watch and no officer to call all hands at first light, the others had overslept. The *Polaris* was theirs now, for better or worse. *Strike that*, thought Owen. *For worse.* And on their very first day, they were already running late—and on a storm-damaged ship, no less.

He swung over the side of his hammock, filling his lungs with the stale air of the cabin. "All hands!" he shouted. "Turn to, you dogs!"

There had been enough slacking in the night. Tragedy, fear, confusion: Whatever the cause, they had already bent enough rules for a lifetime at sea. Captain Eagling was gone. Owen could deny it no longer. But every ship needed a leader, he thought, and there was still some of the Eagling bloodline aboard.

A new day had dawned, and if no one else would do it, Owen was of a mind to crack the whip.

"Come on, forward now," called Owen. "Let's man that pump!"

Henry blinked up at the early morning sun, wiped the sleep from his eyes, and followed the others forward across the deck.

"So we're washing down the deck?" said Thacher.

"Of course!" said Owen.

Henry caught Manny and Mario exchanging quick glances. The crew began every day by washing the deck, a laborious task that could take two hours. Henry was all for cleanliness and routine, but the deck had gotten an extremely thorough washing down in the storm. And that wasn't the only benefit of all that rain.

"The scuttlebutt is full as a ripe berry!" said Aaron.

The barrel of drinking water had been lashed securely to the foremast before the storm, and no one had thought to remove it afterward. Now it was brimming with fresh, clear rainwater. Henry's throat was dry and his mouth was sour, but he hesitated. He knew by now that you never did anything without permission aboard a sailing ship. Was that still the case? And if not, then why was everyone else hesitating too? Could it be as simple as force of habit?

"Drink up, then," said Owen, halting his march toward the seawater pump. "Grab a cup."

Henry held back as the ship's boys rushed the barrel. There were two cups hanging from the side of the barrel on lengths of moldy twine, and he waited as the others gulped down the cool water. His turn finally came, but as soon as he picked up the cup that Aaron had just dropped, Owen called out again: "Enough! You'll drown yourselves!"

The cabin boy turned and resumed his march toward the elm-tree pump, and the others fell in line like ducklings. Henry gulped down half a cupful, coughed, burped, and followed. But once again, he held back as more knowledgeable hands set to work.

The *Polaris* had two pumps: one to pump the bilge water out of the hold and another to pump seawater onto the deck. Henry stared at the latter. It was a marvelous thing, he thought: a hollowed-out tree trunk that went down through the decks and into the ocean below. It was only by the sheer wonder of science—air pressure, water pressure, and equilibrium—that it did not sink the ship immediately.

As Owen grabbed the handle and the Spanish brothers grabbed the buckets, Henry ventured a quick look around the deck. Aaron was standing beside him, staring out over the rail as the sun inched its way above the horizon. The sunlight was straight on, nearly horizontal, and it skipped brightly off the tops of the little wind-tossed waves, turning the face of the sea into an endless field of sparkling diamonds. It astounded Henry that the sea could be so terrifying one moment and so casually beautiful the next.

"You two!" bellowed Owen in between cranks on the pump handle. Henry knew before he even turned around that Owen meant him and Aaron. "Make yourselves useful and grab a swab."

Henry pulled his eyes from the sunrise and looked back at the cabin boy, just to make sure. He got a fierce glare and a *Yes, you!* nod for his trouble. He remembered Owen the night before, benumbed by grief and offering little opinion on anything. He was definitely back to his old bossy self today. *Must not have slept well*, he thought as he and Aaron headed for a little shack on deck. It had once been the goat house, before the poor creature's milk had dried up and they'd eaten her. Now it was where they kept the mops and other instruments of drudgery.

"Is he the captain now?" Henry whispered once they were far enough away.

Aaron turned and looked back at Owen, still cranking away at the pump as seawater began to splash forth, half into the bucket and half onto Mario, who was holding it. Aaron whispered, "Only in his mind." Henry chuckled as Aaron continued. "But he's the best sailor, and I suppose we should listen to him if we don't want to sink."

The smile fell from Henry's face, and for the first time it hit him—really hit him—the situation they were in now. They would have to get this ship to port themselves. He turned and looked back at the others—really looked at them. Children, all of them, not one with any real use for a shaving razor. They had calloused hands and knotty muscles, to be sure, but what experience did any of them have running a ship?

He glanced back over at Aaron. Did he seem a little nervous about it too? Yes, Henry decided, but then, Aaron was always nervous. His job had been carrying gunpowder.

Henry swallowed hard, his throat already gone dry again.

He spent the next two hours pushing an old rope headed mop around the deck. He could see that he was just making things worse. The storm-blasted deck was clean to begin with.

Even the four old cannons, perched vigilantly along the rail, seemed to gleam in the morning light. But the mop was old and moldy, and with the ship riding low in the stirred-up shallows, the seawater in his bucket was gritty with sediment. The little lump of lye soap dissolving inside seemed to do nothing but give it all a toxic smell.

Still, Henry knew better than to point any of this out. He considered himself a scientist, and as such, he learned by careful observation. What he had observed so far in his weeks at sea: Routine trumped common sense every time.

He'd been lucky, in one sense, during those weeks. Death may have fallen all about him like wintry hail, but he'd been spared the endless physical labor aboard the ship. After the doomed expedition had returned, he'd made himself useful by helping the purser out with the ship's logs. In fact, by the end, he'd basically been doing the man's job for him, recording every keg of salt pork, butter, and water opened and every piece of equipment cracked. He hadn't been at all surprised to spot the good-for-nothing purser riding away on the launch among the mutineers.

So now he pushed his old mop without complaint as the others scrambled around doing their share of the chores and maintenance that seemed to occupy every waking moment aboard the ship. Before Dr. Wetherby disappeared into the Amazon, he'd explained it to Henry this way, "A sailing ship is like your Latin: always in need of work." He missed the old doctor so powerfully that even the memory of this insult made Henry's eyes begin to water.

"Hold up," called Manny.

Henry held his swab still as Manny and Mario knelt down in front of him and removed the storm cover from a grating. Once they stood back up, he proceeded to coat the latticework of little wooden squares with grungy seawater. As he did, he peered down through the open squares into the shadowy murk below deck. He remembered the night before: the fear and shifting shadows. That strange smell again. Standing in the morning light, he wanted to dismiss it, to write it all off to the feverish imaginations of the night. But he was a scientist, after all. He learned by careful observation. And at the end, just before they'd fled back up the hatch, he had seen something.

He shivered deeply in the warm morning and pushed his mop quickly across the grate. A quick twirl around the old goat house, back where he'd started, and he was done. He mopped around the old shack once more, for good measure, dreading what he'd be assigned next. *Something shipish and sailory that I'll have no idea how to do, no doubt*, he thought. But when Aaron returned to the shack too, Henry gave up and put his mop away.

For a moment, the two stood side by side in the sun. There were no officers left to call out the time, but dawn was over and it was well and truly morning.

"Must be seven bells by now," said Aaron.

Owen, who was climbing in the rigging ten feet above their heads, either heard him or was thinking the same thing. And seven bells into the morning watch meant one very particular thing on board a working ship. "Who wants to go down to the galley and fetch breakfast?" Owen called down.

Everyone looked around at each other. Henry's eyes flicked back over the grate. The galley was below deck, deep in the ship's shadowy heart.

"Two of you should do," Owen shouted, issuing his orders literally from on high.

No one volunteered, and Henry looked over at Aaron in a slight panic. Was it too late for them to grab their mops and try to look busy again?

"Right!" called Owen. "No breakfast this morning. A dozen rules were broken last night." He paused, and Henry wondered if he would acknowledge his own part in the general disobedience. Instead, he barreled on. "An empty belly seems fit punishment. And it's past time we set sail for home."

As Owen scrambled down the rigging—the angled rope shrouds that kept the masts centered and the horizontal ratlines that turned it all into a vast network of rope ladders—the others exchanged glances again. These looks were different, and Henry saw the hesitation in them. By some unspoken agreement, they'd all consented to accept orders from Owen, at least for now. He was certainly the most experienced sailor: All but raised at sea, he scurried down the ratlines now with the instinctive ease of a monkey on a vine. But he was no older than the rest of them, and it was highly debatable whether he was any wiser.

Manny looked to Mario. Aaron looked to Henry. Thacher stared back up at Owen.

Orders were one thing—but should they really accept punishment from this boy as well?

Owen reached the last ratline, swung down, and landed squarely on the gently rolling deck. His bare feet slapped the freshly swabbed wood, and he turned to face the others. "Work hard and we'll have an early dinner," he said, "when the sun is high overhead."

Everyone nodded. When the sun was high overhead and the sunlight through the grates and hatches was at its brightest. That was when they'd go back down there for their meal.

Suddenly, everyone was in agreement.

"Fair enough," said Thacher.

"I'm not hungry yet, anyway," added Aaron in a lie so obvious that Henry nearly laughed out loud.

The young crew made another trip to the scuttlebutt. A cup of water would be their breakfast. And then it would begin: the complex and grueling set of tasks that went into weighing anchor and setting sail.

The United States of America. The words floated into Henry's head as he dropped the cup and wiped his lips. Still a young nation but already a large one.

He pictured the globe back in Dr. Wetherby's study in Boston. They were on the fat part now, near the equator. They needed to climb the slope, not over a few inches of blue ink and dotted lines but through hundreds of miles of treacherous ocean. He could picture the painted outline of the United States clearly.

If they were ever to set foot on its soil again, this would be their first step.

And if they were to die trying? This would be the first step for that too.

CHAPTER 8

HAULING WIND

"Weigh anchor!" called Owen.

And while Henry admired the brisk can-do tone of the cabin boy's voice, he understood immediately that the problem with weighing anchor was how much an anchor actually weighed. Henry had seen the things splash down into the water, two big double-sided iron hooks that had held firm during the storm. Each one, he was sure, was wedged in firmly and weighed more than all the remaining crew put together.

"Port side first!" called Owen, and Henry remembered the little phrase he'd come up with to remember which side that was. "Just left port," he mumbled to himself, and turned to the left a moment after everyone else.

He took his place on the bow at a large winch known as the windlass, taking hold of its thick rope cable as if preparing for a game of tug-of-war. Being among the lightest, and certainly the weakest, he was jostled into place near the front. Owen took his place on the end. *That makes sense*, thought Henry. *He's the heaviest and has the most bricks in his head.*

At first they hauled in a *one, two, THREE!* rhythm. They got the slack out of the anchor chain without too much trouble, but after that, things ground to a halt. Despite their best efforts—grunts and groans erupting all along the line—the rope barely moved and the windlass stopped turning. Part of the problem was that Henry—not used to this sort of synchronized activity and not very coordinated—always seemed to be half a beat behind.

Henry rubbed his left shoulder—*or port shoulder?* he wondered—as they took a break to reassess.

"It's wedged in good," said Mario. "Could be caught on a reef."

"Or some rocks," offered Manny.

When they went back at it, they used a less elegant method. The three-count was replaced with a simple "Heave! HO!" with everyone falling on their backsides on the second beat. Coordinated or not, Henry could fall on his butt with the best of them.

On the first few tugs, the cable slowly slipped through their hands as they fell to the deck. The rope burn was excruciating.

"AAAH!" hissed Henry, peeling his hands free and shaking them. He looked down at his palms, which had already turned a vicious shade of scarlet.

But a moment later everyone was up again, and Henry scrambled up after them.

"Heave!" called Owen as Henry grabbed on to the cable with tender hands.

"HO!" responded the others, once again pulling with everything they had as they leaned back.

Henry held on tight, despite his burning palms. Up and down the line, the others did the same. And this time, it worked. Instead of his hands slipping painfully down the rope, he felt the rope begin to move. This time, when they fell to the deck, they took half a body length of cable with them. The gears of the windlass engaged and locked in their gains. Henry raised his estimation of the anchor-hauling device from "crude machine" to "technological marvel."

"Again!" called Owen, his voice suddenly upbeat.

This time Henry sprang to his feet, and when he fell to the floor again, it was with a full body length of cable. There was no doubt anymore: The anchor was free from the bottom of the sea.

"Anchor aweigh, boys!" called Owen, and a few of the others cheered.

They resumed their three-count after that, hauling in cable hand over hand. In a mere five fathoms of water, and with the help of the gears of the windlass, it wasn't long before the anchor was snug to the side of the boat. Henry's muscles burned and his hands screamed, but he couldn't help but smile. The anchor was up and he had actually helped. For the first time since he'd taken his initial unsteady footsteps aboard the *Polaris*, he felt like a part of the crew.

"Starboard now!" called Owen, and Henry's smile vanished.

He'd forgotten there was another one. He brushed his burning hands on the soft, worn-out cloth of his pants and prepared to do it all over again.

Aaron and Thacher spat into their hands and rubbed them together, and even that act seemed impressively coordinated to Henry. But the second anchor came up easier, and once again, Henry managed to do his part.

Without a moment's rest, the order was given to set sail, and Henry immediately descended back into uselessness. With a sharp bark of "Lay aloft, you rascals," the others swarmed up into the rigging. Manny and Owen led a breakneck race to the top of the forward mast. Henry was rooting for Manny but didn't see who won, because he was attempting to climb the rigging himself. He put his hands on the shrouds and his feet on the lowest ratline. Then he stepped up onto the next ratline, waited for his foot to sink and settle into the rope, and moved his hands a bit farther up the shroud. He was glad he'd left his boots behind today—bare feet did make it easier. Still, he felt like he could climb all this rope quickly or safely, but not both.

Fifteen feet up, the boat pitched to the side on a gentle swell, and Henry hugged the shrouds and closed his eyes tight. When he opened them again and looked up, he saw the others already at the very top of the mast, spread out across the royal yard. The mast reminded the botanist's assistant of the trunk of a tall, impossibly thin tree. That made the yardarms the even thinner branches—and that made the others climbing across them just plain crazy.

He took his first quick look down, and that was it for him. Even though he was less than a fraction of the way up the mast, the deck already looked far away and bone-crackingly hard. Henry looked up again as the others leaned their chests into the narrow wood of the yard, their feet hooked into the ropes below, and unwrapped the tightly furled sail. "Let fall!" called Owen, and the small, high royal sail cascaded down.

The others quickly descended to the topgallant sail and repeated the process. This time, he just watched them. *I will need to know what to do when I get up there*, he reasoned. He felt useless and guilty, though, and as they went to work on the topsail, Henry resumed his slow creep upward. He went rope by rope, with all the speed and vigor of a drowsy sloth. His problem wasn't a lack of energy, though. His problem was that his heart was pounding like a bass drum in his chest and his hands had begun shaking badly. He inhaled deeply, desperately trying to calm his racing nerves. As he exhaled, he heard Owen bellow, "Let fall!"

Suddenly, the heavy rolls of the mainsail were released, nearly hitting Henry in the head. An avalanche of rustling canvas rushed past, and Henry found himself more or less engulfed by it. Before he could gather himself, he heard a thundering above him and saw the others descending at speeds that seemed halfway between climbing and falling. He hugged the shrouds again as the others jostled past him.

He heard their feet slap the deck one by one as he reversed course and began his careful climb back down. By the time he reached the deck, the others had ropes in their hands again and were hauling still other sails up. He rushed over to grab a rope but couldn't find a spot.

"Joining us, are you?" said Thacher. "How kind of you."

Henry's face burned with embarrassment, but he was pretty sure it was hidden by his sunburn. Aaron shifted his grip and slipped to the other side of the rope to make space for him. Henry mouthed a silent "thank you!" and grabbed hold.

The *Polaris* had two masts, with a swinging menace the others were calling a "trysail" behind the second mast and an assortment of triangular "jibs" in front of the first. It amounted to a vexing assortment of sails. Some of them had to be dropped down, some of them had to be hauled up, and some of them seemed to require both. Baffled by both the words and actions, Henry just tried to find the end of as many ropes as possible and to heave when he was supposed to heave and ho when he was supposed to ho.

He made a dozen mistakes and was sure the others considered him useless. He just hoped Owen hadn't seen the worst of his blunders. With the anchors up and the first sails already bellied out by a stiff morning breeze, Owen had retreated back to the ship's wheel to steer them away from the island and the breaking waves on its not-so-distant shore.

Setting sail with a crew so small, in every sense, was long, hard work. Once it was over, Henry leaned against the railing, huffing and puffing. He looked down at his rubbed-raw hands and then up at the fruits of their labor. The wind wasn't particularly strong—certainly nothing compared to the gale the night before—but with so many sails set, it did the trick. What seemed like acres of pale canvas were puffed out farther than a chipmunk's cheeks in the fall. He could even hear the wind whistling through the rigging.

Henry leaned over the side and saw the bow slicing through the waves and leaving a white wake behind them. Manny wandered by and peered over the side too. "What are you looking at?" asked Manny.

"We're moving nicely," said Henry, pointing at the soft white spray that flew up as the ship sawed through the water.

"Oh," said Manny. "I thought there might be a dolphin or something."

They both scanned the water for a moment, as if looking for one. Then Manny looked up at the full sails. "But, yes, we are hauling wind now."

Henry nodded. He liked that phrase: "hauling wind."

Manny walked away, adding softly, "I just hope we're not hauling too much of it."

Henry looked back up at the sails. The wind whistled. The wood groaned.

An hour later, the burning sun was high overhead. The ship had originally dropped anchor for its fateful, fatal meeting shortly after crossing the equator, and they were still close to that imaginary line around the waist of the world. The sun here was bright and hot, and the days were long.

Henry and Aaron had just taken a grueling turn on the chain pump. This one didn't pump seawater onto the ship but rather bilge water off it: out of its briny bottom, through little grooves in the deck, and over the side. It was bigger than the other pump and located in the waist of the ship, directly over the lowest point in the bilge. It worked with a sort of seesaw mechanism and would have been hard work with two men on each handle. With one boy per side, it was murder.

As they stepped away to let someone else have a go at the pump, Henry's stomach rumbled beneath his sweat-stained shirt. He heard steps behind him but was too worn out to bother turning around to see who it was.

"You! Henry!"

The voice and volume told him it was Owen. He closed his eyes, sucked in a slow breath, and turned around. "Yes?"

"You were useless raising sail this morning," said Owen.

Henry just looked at him. He couldn't exactly deny it. *Thanks for the kick in the britches*, he thought.

"You know that, right?" prodded Owen.

Henry sighed. "I was hoping you wouldn't notice," he said, too tired to lie.

Out of the corner of his eye, he could see a few of the others turning to look his way. Owen broke into a wide smile. Whatever came out of his mouth next, Henry knew, would not be good.

"Now you can make it up to us!" he said.

Henry reached up and dragged the back of his hand across his sweaty forehead, an attempt to point out that he had just taken a long, hard turn on the pump. "Oh yes?" he said. "And how can I do that?"

The others had stopped working now and were staring at him openly. It occurred to him that he was quite possibly the only person on deck who didn't know what was coming next. He was too tired and hungry to think straight. *Hungry*, he thought. *Oh no . . .*

Oh yes.

"You can head below and fetch up dinner for us," said Owen.

"Below?" squeaked Henry. "Alone?"

He winced. He hadn't meant to say that last part aloud.

Owen cocked his head to the side like a curious dog. "How

much do you suppose we'll eat? One person should be more than enough to haul it."

Defeated, Henry allowed his eyes to drift back toward the half-swabbed grating and the darkness underneath. Maybe it wouldn't be so bad now, with daylight leaking through. Maybe it was all in his head. The thought gave him a bit of courage. *Be a scientist*, he told himself. *Be rational.* "Where is it?" he said, straightening up a bit. "How much do I bring?"

"Do you really not know?" said Owen, seeming legitimately surprised.

"In the galley?" Henry ventured. He knew he should know this, and he didn't want to get it wrong with everyone watching. "Or, wait, the pantry?"

Owen's fake smile settled into an authentic smirk. "Useless," he murmured.

Off to his left, Manny chuckled lightly—and at exactly the wrong time. Owen raised his left hand and pointed toward the sound. "You," he said. "Spaniard. Go with him. Make sure he doesn't bring us lamp oil for lunch."

"Aah! But! Why? I-I-" Manny stammered.

Owen's smile returned. "I suppose we could wait till this evening to eat . . ."

"No!" blurted Thacher and Mario at the same moment.

Manny turned and glared at Mario: *Even you?*

"Fine," Manny said, and then spat disdainfully onto the deck.

I just swabbed that deck, thought Henry, falling in line behind Manny as they headed toward the aft hatch.

Manny turned and looked at him. "You are just useless," said the Spaniard, the soft, swooping accent making the harsh words sound elegant and almost feminine.

"I'm not *just* useless," protested Henry.

"Oh no? Then what else are you?"

"I'm useless," clarified Henry, "and scared too."

A quick smile flashed across Manny's face as they reached the hatch and started down the ladder. "Then we have something in common."

Henry took one last breath of clean salt air and then headed below. Work resumed on deck as the two descended into the deep shadows. There was a pool of sunlight at the base of the ladder, and when Henry reached the bottom, Manny stepped aside just enough to let Henry stand in it as well.

"That's not good," said Manny, pointing forward.

Henry blinked a few times as his eyes adjusted to the dim light beyond. The lantern they'd relied on the night before lay smashed on the floor, surrounded by a pool of oil.

"It must have fallen from its hook in one of the swells," said Manny.

"That's unlikely," said Henry, considering it. The thing had stayed on its hook through the mountainous waves of the storm.

Why would it fall during the modest swells that followed? But if it wasn't the swells that knocked it down . . . "Oh," he said.

Manny looked at him very seriously and then repeated the words slowly and clearly: "It must have fallen from its hook in one of the swells."

This time Henry didn't argue.

"We'll have to replace it," added Manny. "We can take the one from the galley."

Henry peered into the shadowy distance in front of them. He swallowed loudly.

Manny stared straight ahead and took one tentative step out of the circle of light, then another.

Be a scientist, Henry urged himself, and followed.

CHAPTER 9

A NOISE IN THE DARKNESS

Manny peered at the path ahead. The sailors called this the between deck, located as it was between the sunlit main deck above and the ship's dark and cavernous hold below. It was between daylight and darkness, and the two mixed uneasily here. Moving slowly away from the stern of the ship, Manny and Henry entered a dark space in between the hatch and the first grating.

Should they speed up to get through the darkness faster, wondered Manny, or slow down, move carefully, and listen? The sound of Henry stumbling clumsily in the dark provided the answer. Slow, it was.

Manny took slow, shallow breaths and felt the weight of the world closing in, with a chest that felt constricted beneath two layers of shirts and a head that pounded beneath the tight black cloth wrapped around it. The Spanish style . . . Ha! No Spaniard with any sense would wear extra layers on the equator!

Eyes wide open, ears alert, they crept forward. They reached the grating, its light hitting the floor in a checkerboard pattern. Manny exhaled. They reached the crew berth, and its cluttered expanse was all that stood between them and the galley. At least, they hoped that was the only thing standing in their way.

They stepped carefully over dead men's boots and sea trunks. The smell of sweat and chewing tobacco still hung heavily in the air, but it was better than the ghostly, unnatural sweetness. They reached the galley. The door hung half open, a faint light radiating from inside. Manny's heart pounded. Henry gulped down foul air.

"Come on, let's get this over with," Manny growled, slapping the door with an open palm.

The door swung open and smacked the wall. A moment later, as if in response, a second thump sounded from somewhere in the darkness. Manny whirled around but saw only Henry's face, his mouth formed into a big round O and his eyes almost as wide.

"What was that?" Henry said, pointing farther down the passage. "It came from somewhere up there."

Manny grabbed him by the shirt, pulled him inside the galley, and then slammed the thin wooden door behind them. But their troubles would not be shut out so easily.

The door slammed: *PAK!*

It was followed immediately by another sound from out in the passage: *BRONK!*

Was that closer, thought Manny, *or just louder?*

Henry stammered out a series of half thoughts: "But . . . what . . . is there someone . . . no, but . . ."

"Let's just get the food," said Manny, drawing some thin comfort from the closed door and the light streaming in from above them. The galley had its own small grating, more for venting the cooking smoke than for letting light in, but it served both purposes.

"Take that down," said Manny, pointing to a grimy old lantern hanging from a hook on the wall.

As Henry reached up for it, Manny bent to tip a barrel of salt pork. If it wasn't too full, they could take the whole— "EEEEEEEEEE!" screamed Manny, high-pitched and loud, as a dark shape bolted out from behind the barrel.

Henry gasped and fell back, juggling the lantern in both hands as if it had suddenly come alive.

There was a scrabble of claws on wood, digging in, gaining traction, and then the quick thump of small footsteps.

"Daffy!" cried Manny.

Henry finally gained control of the elusive lantern. He let out a long breath and said, "You're kidding me."

Daffodil, the ship's cat, reached the door. Finding it closed, she spun around to face the intruders. Her eyes glowed faintly in the shadows. As soon as she identified the newcomers, she settled onto her haunches and began to clean herself, unconcerned.

"Bad cat!" huffed Manny. "*¡Gato malo!*"

Another strange sound filled the little galley, and it took Manny a while to realize that it was Henry, laughing softly.

"What's so funny?"

"You," he said, adding a quick imitation of Manny's scream: "EEEEEE!"

He kept the volume down but got the pitch right. Manny burned with embarrassment.

"You sounded like a girl," said Henry.

As fast as a hawk in flight, Manny turned and took two quick steps toward Henry. Henry immediately stumbled backward, holding the lantern in front of himself for protection.

"Another word, and I'll leave you down here!" spat Manny.

"But—" Henry began.

"Unconscious!"

The two stared at each other in the dim light. Henry's eyes were confused and unfocused, but Manny's blazed with intensity.

"All right, fine," said Henry, looking down. "Cripes."

"Here," said Manny, suddenly eager to change the subject. "Take this tin of sea bread, that jar of molasses, and anything else that looks halfway edible. This barrel of meat is less than half full—must be pork, since that's what we've been having the last few days. Anyway, I can carry it myself."

They loaded up and turned back toward the door. Daffodil waited at their feet, her tail flicking back and forth, nose pressed to the edge of the door.

"Why are we taking so much stuff?" asked Henry, the lantern balanced atop a fat packet of beef jerky that was itself stacked on top of two tins of the hard, flat biscuits known as sea bread. The jar of molasses was pinned under his arm.

Manny looked at him like he was an idiot. "Do you want to come back down here again anytime soon?"

"Oh, right," said Henry. He opened his mouth again, but for a long moment, nothing came out. Manny knew instantly that he was considering another stupid question.

"You know this ship better than I do," he said. "Do you think that noise—those noises—could have been Daffodil? Maybe she knocked something over?"

Manny stared at him again, thinking, *That would be quite a trick, considering that she was asleep behind this barrel I'm holding.* But then a second thought: *What if she hadn't been sleeping? What if she'd been hiding?*

But Henry was scared enough, and Manny was sick of questions.

"*Es posible,*" said Manny with a shrug. It's possible.

True or not, the words were enough to prompt Henry to open the door and head back into the murky passage. Daffodil darted between his feet, nearly upending him.

The air that had been so stale and foul before they entered the galley was now laced with the faintest hint of sweetness. The two exchanged looks and sped up, barely looking down as they hustled through the darkness. Manny kicked a fallen hat across the crew berth without consequence only to painfully stub a toe on a misplaced sea trunk. They reached the hatch in record time, just as Daffodil's tail disappeared up the last rung of the angled ladder and out onto the deck. They replaced the fallen lantern and headed up after her. But Henry went first and his progress was painfully slow. He had the lighter load and even one hand partially free, but he lacked the Spaniard's talent for climbing.

"Hurry up!" hissed Manny.

If there was another noise behind them—so much as the scritch-scratch of a rat along the wall—Manny vowed to climb right over this bookish boy's back. But there was only silence as they made their agonizingly slow ascent. Silence and the vague, unnerving, and all-too-familiar sense of being watched.

CHAPTER 10

COMING UNWRAPPED

With a heavy thud, Manny dropped the barrel of salted meat onto the deck and then breathed in the fresh sea air, blinking into the blinding sunlight. The scene on deck slowly came into view. Aaron was standing at the helm behind them, taking his turn at the big wooden wheel, steering the ship. As usual, Manny sought out Mario—and instantly recoiled in horror. "Mario! What are you doing?"

Mario looked over and continued slowly unwrapping the black headscarf. "I'm sick of this thing."

"But—but—" Manny stammered.

"But nothing. My brains are boiling."

"But you must leave it!" Manny's eyes were wild, staring at Mario and then casting quick, worried glances around at the others. "You know it's the Spanish style!"

Mario snorted out a laugh. "That's not even a real thing. And even if it were, you know that's not why we wear these."

The others had all turned to look, and the headscarf was almost off now, the sweat-soaked black cloth drooping heavily as it came free. Manny panicked and switched to Spanish. *"Sí, lo sé, pero los otros no saben."* Yes, I know, but the others don't.

Mario looked around at all the gawking eyes and shrugged. *"¿A quién le importa?"* Who cares? Then, in English: "It's just us now: no officers, no old salts. Just us children, so what does it matter what kind?"

Manny forced a small laugh, as if not understanding. *"En español, por favor."*

"No," said Mario.

Manny glared. "Don't you dare!"

"Too late!" said Mario, unwrapping the final layer and exposing the thick, damp black hair underneath.

Manny stepped deftly around the barrel and rushed toward Mario, who darted back with all the grace and ceremony of a Spanish bullfighter. With a flourish, Mario tugged the damp headscarf up and away from Manny's grasping hands. The others howled and hooted with delight.

Panic and anger flooded Manny's mind. "Maria, no!"

The deck fell silent.

For a few moments, the only sounds were the wind whistling through the sails and the waves slapping against the hull. Henry broke the silence: "Did he say *Maria*?"

Manny made another lunge at the cloth, this time with a threat: "I'll wrap it around your stupid neck!"

But the other "Spanish brother" spun aside once more, long, wavy black hair twirling out and then falling heavily down. And even the face that hair now framed looked different, no longer tightly cropped by austere black cloth, with a few weeks' worth of grime having washed off in the storm the night before.

All around the pair, the others stood and stared in silent disbelief. What a difference a blurted name and an unwrapped headscarf made. The truth had been hiding in plain sight all along.

Maria broke the silence. "Don't you see? We don't have to pretend anymore, Emma."

Emma, short for Emmanuelle, groaned: "Do I see? *Everyone* sees now."

She looked down at her own sunburned feet, not yet daring to meet the eyes of the others, and retraced the steps that had led here. This whole thing had been her idea: a simple disguise in exchange for a steady job and a ticket to a new life. That was the idea, anyway. Emma looked sheepishly up at her sister. And now, after more than a year of hard labor, serious secrets, and uncomfortable camouflage, Maria couldn't resist a little payback. She batted her eyelashes at Emma—playfully, girlishly, and just for fun.

Owen closed his eyes tightly, but when he opened them, the view still hadn't changed at all. *Had Mario's eyelashes always been that long?* he asked himself. *Wait, I mean, Maria's?*

"So let me get this straight," said Thacher. "Let me see if I have it figured . . ."

"It appears," said Henry, cutting in with a schoolmaster's tone that annoyed Owen, "that two of the ship's boys are actually—"

"Ship's girls," said Owen, who could cut in with the best of them.

Aaron called up from the wheel, demanding to know what was going on.

"It's still your trick at the helm!" Owen called back. Then he turned to the Spanish sisters and lowered his voice: "He's not the only one awaiting an explanation."

"Yes, fine," said Emma with an exasperated sigh. "I'll explain if you all stop staring." She waited a moment, but the eyes stayed on her. Another sigh, and then: "We had no life back in Spain: no parents, no money. Other orphans made their way to Barcelona and found work on the ships, but they would not hire girls, or even women. It is stupid, of course. Most people don't think things through—and most people don't look too closely at the things right in front of them. And so I came up with a plan . . ."

"It's bad luck!" blurted Owen. "Women on board a ship: Everyone knows it's bad luck!"

"It is a silly superstition," said Maria flatly.

Owen felt his sunburned face getting hotter still. He refused to be lectured by these girls! "That's probably why all of this has happened!" The words came out in a rush, the thought suddenly occurring to him. "The mutiny, the—the—"

"The what?" said Emma, her expression turning scornful. "The ghost?"

Owen looked down, suddenly embarrassed by what he'd been about to say, and Emma continued on. "There is something down there," she said, pointing straight down at the deck. "We all know that." She gestured at Henry. "And we heard it. But it is no ghost. It is alive, and as solid as any of us. And as for the mutiny, well . . ."

She let the thought hang there as she slowly looked around at the others, knowing no one would cut her off this time. "Well, I think maybe they knew something about it that we do not."

"But how?" said Owen. "What?"

"*No sé*," said Emma with a shrug. "I don't know. But I have heard talk of many bloody mutinies. I have heard of the losing side being set adrift in longboats. But never, ever have I heard of men taking control of a ship only to abandon it."

Owen nodded. It had been bothering him too. "And trying to blow it up behind them," he added.

"Exactly," said Emma. "So maybe it wasn't the ship they were trying to get away from."

"And perhaps it wasn't the ship they were trying to blow up," added Henry.

The crew fell silent again. The gears ground slowly in Owen's head, and once again he wished he were more clever. He briefly wished that he were more like Henry, but a quick glance at the other boy's scrawny frame and slumped posture brought him back to himself. Not *too much* like Henry.

"I think they were overcome with guilt for what they'd done," said Maria, breaking the spell. "They knew they'd be hanged when they reached port."

Thacher nodded. "Yes, could be they planned to sink the ship and then claim to have survived a shipwreck. As for what lurks below deck, a ghost is much more likely."

"Well then," said Emma, pointing back toward the aft hatch. "I invite you to go down there and find out for yourself."

Owen turned to see where she was pointing, but his eyes never reached the hatch. They locked onto the barrel of salted meat directly in front of it. Then he saw the food Henry had dropped beside it. His stomach rumbled.

"I have a better idea," he said.

CHAPTER 11

THE WIND AT THEIR BACKS

In the past, with the full crew divided up into four-hour watches and then divided up again into two-hour dogwatches, they ate in shifts at the little table in the galley. Cutlery, cups, maybe even a rag for a napkin. Now the new crew ate with their hands in the bright openness of the sunlit deck.

Aaron had been a friend and occasional assistant to the ship's cook, and he'd had no trouble boiling the salt pork in a little kettle they'd found stowed in the former goat house. The kettle was meant more for heating tar than boiling food, but with meat of this quality, there wasn't a huge difference. Not that any of them complained. Each crew member received a slab of the stuff, salted to near oblivion in order to prevent it from spoiling during the trip. To go with it, they each got a dry, flat biscuit. And to wash down this dry, salty feast: a few gulps of water from the scuttlebutt.

Most of them took their time. Meals were often the only true breaks in a sailor's day. They savored the chance to rest, if not the meal. A few of them ate quickly, though, too hungry from a long day with no food. Owen had always had a big appetite, but looking around he saw that Thacher had him beat. The hold rat had already gobbled down his hunk of salted meat and was licking his lips for any scraps. *Ravenous as a wolf,* he thought.

As Thacher rubbed his hands on his grimy pants, he raised his eyes and caught Owen sizing him up. Owen wasn't the sort to look away quickly, to pretend it hadn't happened, and so for a moment they held each other's gaze. Thacher lifted his chin toward the spot where the barrel of salt pork was resting near the mainmast. Owen shook his head: No. They might eat like savages, sprawled out on the deck, but there would be no seconds. Thacher gave him a sour smirk and looked away.

Owen made a mental note to stow the food away after they finished. He glanced up at the raised forecastle. In larger ships, the fo'c'sle was where the crew slept, but it was far too low for that on the *Polaris*. Instead, it served as a convenient place to store ropes and sailcloth and anything else they might need quickly. It would keep the food out of the sun, and out of sight.

"You better save some of that for me!" Aaron called up from the wheel.

Owen looked back at him and then right back at Thacher.

"You were on the same dogwatch as Aaron, were you not?"

Thacher looked up and gave the smallest of nods.

"Then go relieve him," said Owen. "It's your trick."

"But I haven't finished yet," said Thacher, holding up a small scrap of sea bread as proof.

"And he hasn't started," Owen shot back.

Thacher made a show of getting up, moving in a slow, pained way. As he did, he leaned over and muttered something to Henry. The gusty wind died down once more, and Owen heard the words clearly.

"Who died and made him captain?"

The words hit Owen in the gut, stirring up a swirl of anger and sorrow. He shot them both a look. Henry looked down immediately, but this time it was Thacher who refused to look away. He smiled back. "What?" he said, his voice dripping with fake innocence.

Owen played out the exchange in his head. *He wants me to repeat it, to say what I heard.* He glared back at Thacher. *I won't do it; I won't defame my captain's memory.* "Watch yourself, hold rat," he said.

Thacher's smile fell away and his expression darkened. "I think we should all watch ourselves now," he said, his tone ice cold despite the burning sun.

"Is that a threat?" said Owen.

"It's a fact," said Thacher as he turned on his heel and headed for the wheel.

Owen looked around at the others as if to say, *You all heard that, right?* But no one said anything until Aaron flopped down on the deck with his food a few moments later. Henry turned to him immediately and pointed over at Emma and Maria. "They're girls!" he said.

Aaron's mouth fell open, and a little spray of sea bread crumbs rained down onto his lap. His surprise was so immediate and genuine that everyone except Owen laughed.

"I'm Maria."

"And I'm Emma," they said, introducing themselves to their old friend for the first time.

Emma's hair was down now too, and Owen saw it fly out behind her in a quick gust of wind.

As it did, the ship rose up abruptly and slammed down with a heavy crash. Owen looked up toward the bow and saw white spray clear the railing on both sides. He shouted back over his shoulder, "Ease her as she pitches, Thacher! The wind is picking up, and the waves with it!"

As the others chattered about the sisters' secret and laughed at "the Spanish style" and their own gullibility, Owen fell back into his own thoughts. Henry claimed to have known all along and was roundly hooted down. Owen ignored the noise and looked up into the sails.

The wind is definitely stronger now, he thought. It had been no more than a steady breeze that morning, and they'd set every sail they had to catch every puff of it. But now the wind was no longer in such short supply, and the gusts were driving them forward hard. He tried to tune out the chatter all around him and listen. Another gust and he heard the wood of the mainmast groan from somewhere up high. He squinted skyward into the topsail, but before he could find the source of the sound, another groan from the foremast drew his attention.

As he looked up, he relied on his other senses as well. He sat heavily on his haunches, feeling the ship rushing forward beneath him, smashing down the waves as it went. *Small*, he thought, *but growing*. He gazed up toward the bow and waited for the *Polaris* to crest a larger wave. He didn't have to wait long. As the big boat crashed down, he felt the impact shoot up his spine and ring his skull like a bell.

He gulped down his last dirt-dry mouthful of sea bread and looked around.

This time it was Emma who met his gaze. "Think we should reef some of the sails?" she said.

It was exactly what he'd been wondering. Shortening some of the sail would reduce the amount of wind they hauled and be easier on the ship. It was the prudent thing to do. The others hated the idea immediately.

"Are you joking?" said Henry. "This wind is wonderful. The faster we get to port, the better."

Owen ignored his words utterly—he was no sailor.

"Nothing more than some afternoon gusts," said Maria with a shrug.

Owen tried to ignore that too. What did she know of the weather?

"The ship has been through much worse," said Aaron evenly.

"Yes, much worse," agreed Owen. "But not at full sail."

Aaron glanced up nervously.

"A few gusts, nothing more," repeated Maria before pushing further. "And we're lucky to have them." She paused. "We are still near the equator, no?"

"Yes," admitted Owen. He knew where she was going with this and decided to get there first. "And still prone to the doldrums."

The hot, windless stretches known as the doldrums had plagued them on the voyage out, leaving them drifting helplessly for days at a time. Owen remembered the frustration etched on the faces of captain and crew, a speedy trip ruined, the sea seeming to turn to syrup beneath them.

He paused too long in the memory, and the others redoubled their protests.

"We have a good wind at our backs," said Henry. "The most logical approach is to take advantage of it."

Owen didn't care for the boy's seamanship, but if he was being completely honest, he was somewhat intimidated by Henry's scientific education. Logical. He nodded.

"I wish to get to port as soon as possible," said Aaron. "Even a few puffs earlier would be welcome."

Emma looked around at the others. "We all want to reach

port," she said. "This ship is an awful place now. But sailing it alone will not be easy, and we have to be smart—and maybe cautious too." She turned to face Owen. "Tell us what you think we should do, and I'll abide by it."

The others either nodded or mumbled their agreement. Owen took a deep breath and another look up into the tightly stretched sails. It was up to him now. A stray thought flitted across his mind like a sparrow flashing across a cloudy sky. The old crew had never liked him much—the captain's nephew. Wouldn't it be nice if this new one did? He tried to bat the thought away and concentrate on the ship.

The *Polaris* rocked beneath them, the wind whistled through the sails, and the wooden masts groaned out their opinion on the matter. Owen heard them, but they were good thick masts, as wide as trees at their bases, and they'd been well greased and maintained.

He looked up at the sky. Not a dark cloud in sight. With the words of the others still fresh in his mind—a few afternoon gusts, a good wind at our backs—he spoke.

"Full sail," he said. Henry, Maria, and Aaron cheered. He went on: "The wind is fickle in these waters. We'll keep a close eye on it, but I fear that before long we'll be complaining of too little wind rather than too much."

The crew finished their last bites of food and rose to their feet as one, finding the deck a bit more wobbly beneath them than it had been when they sat down. It was a fine speech, but as they headed back to work, Emma took a few steps closer to Owen. "Are you sure?" she said.

Owen angled his steps away from her, still slightly unsettled by the idea of girls on board. He frowned. "Fairly sure," he said, though even that was overstating it.

"With all the sails set, one big gust and—"

"And we'll take some in," he said.

"If you say so," she said, and then she brightened. "We are making good time, no doubt."

Owen smiled too, remembering the old sailor she'd picked up that "no doubt" from. Her English had been almost nonexistent when she first joined the crew, but it had been acquired in such close quarters with so many for so long, and it was still dotted with the sayings of many of those men. But it was an innocent phrase all her own that knocked the smile from his face.

"If you are sure of our course," she continued, "we could reach port ahead of schedule. Imagine it, ahead of schedule, despite all this foul luck."

"If you are sure of our course . . ." He looked back at Thacher at the wheel and then dipped his hand into his vest pocket. So far from shore, he'd replaced the borrowed spyglass with the captain's compass. He turned it over in his hand now and felt its weight.

CHAPTER 12

SPRINGING THE YARD

Owen leaned over a well-worn map spread out across the desk in the corner of the captain's cabin. Sunlight poured in from the windows, heating the side of his face and illuminating his predicament. He squinted down at the map, taking in all the markings. The black lines across the blue ocean denoted depth and currents and dangerous reefs. He eyed the less exact marks that had been left by the captain himself—the dotted lines and circled Xs—favored routes for a trip made many times.

He traced one route in particular with his hand, his fingertips skimming hundreds of miles of imaginary sea in seconds. He followed the Central American coast northward and then veered off slightly to shoot the gap between the Yucatán Peninsula and Cuba. His eyes darted from side to side as he went, taking in the little arrows that indicated the direction of the currents flowing through the Caribbean Sea. His finger cut east and then northward, along the U.S. coast. He tapped it twice: home.

This is the route we're on. He glanced up at the compass, suspended in a gyroscopic gimbal at the top of the desk. *Isn't it?* He looked back down at the map. *These are the currents we need to follow . . . Aren't they?*

The truth was, he had been no more than an occasional fly on the wall as the captain and first mate fussed over the maps and charts, debating winds, currents, and compass readings. He had certainly never taken part—well, unless you counted holding the captain's tea as he worked the divider, or bringing a lamp a bit closer to some chart or other. Still, he felt confident he was doing it right—he had Eagling blood in him after all.

He went over it all one more time. Once again, he became engrossed in the scaled-down world of the map. He didn't notice that the sunlight was failing, the view through the window behind him turning from gold to gray. Nor did he hear the soft sound of something sneaking up on him.

The door still hung lightly off its busted hinges, that morning's hasty repair having failed just as quickly. As Owen hunched over the little desk, a dark shadow slipped silently in through the gap.

It slid across the room, staying low, heading straight for his leg.

Merew, it said, brushing against him.

He felt the cat's fur against the side of his bare ankle and reached down. But Daffodil sped away before he could pet her. "Well, then why did you rub my leg in the first place, you beast?"

The ship's cat jumped up onto the captain's narrow bed, which now had a few charts spread out across the neatly tucked red blanket, along with the captain's well-thumbed copy of Bowditch's *Practical Navigator*. Daffodil nosed the pillow and looked back over at Owen. *Mew?*

"Yes," he said softly. "I miss him too." He looked down at the big map, devilish in its complexity. "How I miss him."

The two considered each other. The ship's cat was technically the property of the captain, and the cabin boy was, if not his property, at least his servant. Owen's heart cracked ever so slightly as Daffodil lay down on the captain's pillow. *Only his scent remains . . .*

Suddenly, a loud thump sounded against the wall of the cabin. Owen looked over toward the wall, and back toward the window. The strong sunlight was gone now, the view much darker. *When did that happen?* The ship pitched forward, and he held on to the sides of the desk. As he tried to rise from his chair, a second, much stronger thump knocked him onto his backside.

The weather had turned, and the ship was being buffeted by strong gusts of wind.

Daffodil sprang to the floor and scampered under the bed. A moment later, a horrible groan sounded from out on deck, as loud as a dying cow. Before Owen could even push his chair back and stand, the sound transformed into a sharp and thunderous *KRACKK!*

"Oh no," he mumbled.

He rushed across the room and toward the busted door, knowing in his pounding heart that he was already too late.

Wedging his way through, he looked into the darkening skies above. He knew what he'd find, but not where he'd find it. Gazing into the sails, he saw it instantly.

The mainmast . . . Blast it all.

"We've sprung the yard," said Emma.

He glared at her, searching her tone for any little bit of "I told you so." Not finding any, he relented. "I can see that," he said. "Come on, then. Let's get up there before the whole thing comes down."

The two rushed across the deck, picking up Aaron, Thacher, and Maria as they went. Aaron had been pulling apart old rope with Henry, showing him how to make the little bits of oakum they used to plug gaps in the wood. When Aaron stood up, Henry did also, but Owen could see he didn't know what was going on. He took one look at Henry's baffled expression and hesitant half steps and called, "You stay down here and take the wheel! It's too dangerous aloft till we get that sheet down."

Too dangerous for a landlubber, anyway, he thought.

A glint of steel at Henry's feet caught his eye. "But hand me that knife!"

Henry reached down and held it out, the blade straight toward Owen's grasping hand. "Handle first, lubber!" he yelled at Henry, angry that he'd had to break his stride and wait. "Are you trying to gut me?"

Henry flipped the blade around clumsily, nearly cutting both of them in the process. Owen grabbed it, secured it between his teeth, and hopped up onto the railing. He didn't so much as glance down at the boundless depths below. Instead, he swung himself up into the lowest ratlines and began his swift climb upward.

As Owen got higher, he could see the extent of the damage. The yardarm that held the big square mainsail was cracked, and the end on the port side was drooping noticeably. With each gust of wind, the wood splintered further. The fibrous sound of wood pulling itself apart made Owen sicker than the sea ever had.

Stupid, stupid, stupid, stupid, he thought. He should have known this would happen. Sailing was always a dance with the devil, but these seas packed particular perils at this time of year, when hot air and cooler waters could produce devastating winds literally out of the blue.

In their eagerness to get home sooner, they'd set too much sail. *Stupid*. He clamped down hard on the blade between his teeth, tasting metal and then blood. *So stupid*. He climbed faster, channeling his anger and pulling ahead of the others.

When he reached the yard, he began scooting his way out on it. As he advanced, he could feel it giving up under his weight, every little crack and pop in the busted wood. Reluctantly, he put his feet back in the ratlines. He took the knife from his mouth.

"Sprung," he called back. "Utterly sprung—take care."

For a moment, he thought he'd have to cut the whole thing down, but a few large gashes in the canvas relieved some of the pressure. He replaced the knife and began taking the big sail down. The other four worked alongside him to do the same. He looked over at Emma, remembering her words clearly: "Are you sure?"

She had been right, and he owed her an apology—or at least an acknowledgment of the fact. Instead, he just shook his head as if to say, *Can you believe this wind?* He found himself grateful for the knife in his mouth, which cut him off before he could begin to speak.

The crew worked hard and carefully to unfasten the big sail. The boat pitched and rolled in the sudden wind, and Henry's inexpert steering didn't help. The motion was exaggerated as they hung from the mast high above the deck. They braced themselves as another powerful gust of wind filled the flapping, snapping sail and nearly carried them all away. Owen reached down and gashed the thing a few more times. He imagined he was stabbing an enemy, a mutineer.

With ten hands working quickly, the big mainsail—the largest on the ship—soon came down.

"Heads up down there," Owen called to Henry. "Don't get tented."

But the wind carried the heavy canvas forward as it fell to the deck, far from Henry's post at the wheel. Thacher and Emma raced down to secure it as it hung up on the loose edges of the deck and kicked up and rippled in the wind.

Maria and Aaron descended with their usual speed. But Owen climbed down slowly, checking for any further damage and thinking about what would come next. If they'd had a full crew—including the carpenter and his assistant—they would have tried to replace the sprung yard with one of the spare spars below. But with a skeleton crew and both of those men at the bottom of the sea? He looked down toward the deck and saw Thacher and Emma wrestling clumsily with the torn mainsail. Were they . . . *laughing*?

It was hopeless. They would have to limp home without the largest sail on the ship. Stunned by the sheer and sudden weight of their misfortune, he swore, nicking his tongue on the knife. He spat the thing out without so much as a "Look out below!" His mouth pooled with blood, and he spat that out too.

Thacher poked his head out from below the undulating canvas on deck. "Should we start mending it?" he called up. He poked his hand through one of the knife wounds. "You've made bloody work of it!"

Owen dropped his head, spat out another mouthful of blood, and called out, "You can throw it overboard for all I care. The mainsail will stay bare."

The others turned to stare up at him.

Thacher's hand was still poking playfully through the hole in the canvas, but his face was now utterly stricken. "What was that?" he said, though he'd clearly heard him.

"Are you sure?" called Aaron.

Owen had heard those words before. But this time he was sure. What did they know about replacing yards? It was a job for seasoned carpenters. It would be dangerous to try—and more dangerous to do wrong. He pictured falling lumber bashing down on deck or tearing through the rigging.

"I'm sure," he said. "Someone fetch me the saw, and I will cut this broken wood off myself."

Owen sawed furiously, channeling his anger into his strokes. Sawdust slipped free and was immediately scattered by the gusting winds. "Careful down there," he called as the saw's teeth worked their way through the cracked wood. But he timed the final stroke perfectly and the port-side end of the old spar broke free just as the ship listed that way. The severed shaft plunged safely into the sea, where it bobbed back to the surface and was immediately caught up in the ship's wake. It clunked against the hull—once, twice—as if in protest. And then it was gone, lost to the vast ocean they'd already put behind them.

The sky had darkened by the time Owen returned to deck, and so had the mood of the crew. Owen could hear their occasional mutterings all around him. He watched as Thacher leaned in to whisper something to Aaron and they both looked over at him. A few minutes later, he turned to see Maria giving him a particularly venomous glare. He didn't even dare look in Emma's direction.

They blame me, he thought, and for a fleeting moment, he almost did too.

But as he stowed the saw and his tongue refused to heal, he remembered other words. Not just "Are you sure?" but also "This wind is wonderful" and "The faster we get to port, the better" and "Even a few puffs earlier would be welcome."

He remembered, in fact, every single word the others had said to him. He remembered "a few puffs, nothing more" and Maria's sly insinuation of the doldrums. He turned to glare back at her now, but she was bent over her work. It was getting a bit dark for meaningful glares anyhow.

With his pride hurt and the coppery taste of his own blood still in his mouth, he convinced himself it was the others' fault. *Once again, I did exactly what they wanted*, he thought, *even when I should have known better. I have to stop listening to these people!*

He spat a red gob onto the deck and glared around at them, daring them to say anything. They didn't, though. They were too tired from reefing the remaining sails. And Thacher, who might normally have been counted on for a barbed comment or two, had relieved Henry at the wheel before he bashed the ship to pieces on the growing waves.

Owen looked up. He saw the shortened sails bellied out in the dying light. But more than that, he saw the dark gap where the mainsail should've been. From now on they'd be limping home with a hole in their very middle, the old ship slower and harder to maneuver than ever.

As the first fat drops of rain began to fall, Owen thought that this was as bad as it could get.

He had no way of knowing that the real danger wasn't looming in the growing darkness above his head but lurking in the shadowy hollows below his feet.

And that like the darkness, it was growing.

And like the sky, it was changing.

CHAPTER 13

A NEW ORDER

The squall passed quickly, scooting off to the west and taking its treacherous winds with it. It had wasted no time doing its damage, with a leading edge packing gusts that would have been right at home in a hurricane. As the new crew dried out, the watch was set for the first time.

"The ship can't sail itself," said Owen after a silent supper of salt pork and sea bread.

"And we cannot sail it either," he heard someone whisper. Thacher, he figured, but it was too dim to know for sure. There were a few chuckles in response, and those were harder to ignore.

"Half of us need to be on deck at all times overnight," he said, raising his voice. "There aren't enough of us for dogwatches."

Owen took charge of the first watch without asking, and Emma was voted head of the second watch. The two best sailors, Owen thought with some satisfaction, but he wondered if that was still the consensus of the others. They picked their sides as if choosing teams for a game of rounders.

Owen picked Aaron first, not because he was the most skilled seaman but because he was the most cautious. *Perhaps he will keep us from sinking the boat altogether*, he thought sullenly as he made the pick. Emma chose Maria, to no one's great surprise. Owen could see no sensible alternative and was forced to choose Thacher. That left Emma stuck with Henry.

"We will make a sailor out of you yet, just watch," she said, trying to make the best of it.

The captain's cabin was less crowded that night, with half of them out on deck. Owen piled the spare maps and a few particularly sharp pieces of navigation equipment on the captain's bed, afraid that someone would take a cat nap there while he was on deck. Someone other than the actual cat, anyway. Since joining them, Daffodil hadn't returned to her old haunts below deck. Instead, she mostly paced the deck and napped in the cabin.

"She don't like it down there either," said Aaron.

"We are spoiling her rotten with scratches behind the ear and bits of pork," said Owen, ignoring the fact that he was, at that moment, scratching her behind the ear.

"I have heard it said that cats are unusually sensitive to ghostly phenomena and hauntings," said Thacher. "Dogs as well."

"Cats are definitely very sensitive to dogs," said Owen, intentionally misunderstanding.

Thacher blew out a puff of air, though it was unclear if it was from laughter or disdain. "You heard what Manny—I mean, the girl—had to say. Doors slamming in the dark, the lantern shattered upon the floor . . ."

"Ships roll, doors slam," said Owen.

There was silence as the three swung lightly in their hammocks, and then Thacher said in a strange, sing-songy voice, "Ships roll, doors slam, and Owen stays above deck with the rest of us."

Owen could have responded angrily—he thought he probably should have—but instead he laughed. It was true. He kept denying it, and yet he was avoiding going between decks as much as any of them. And anyway, it felt good to laugh.

Aaron joined in, and then, with a soft, dry chuckle, so did Thacher.

We don't have to be enemies, thought Owen. *It doesn't have to be like that.* And then he drifted off for a few hours of restless sleep. His nightmares were built mostly of his memories: cracked masts, bodies tossed overboard, and the dark corners between decks. He woke up near dawn to the jarring blows of the ship smashing crossways into the waves. He knew without needing to look that it must be Henry's turn at the wheel.

Over the next several days, the skies stayed clear and the winds held up. The ship continued its steady progress up into the Caribbean. As the ship made the most of its remaining sails, the crew took advantage of the relative calm.

Aaron took it upon himself to teach Henry what he could of seamanship. Owen saw the two of them talking and even laughing as they pushed their mops around and fussed over frayed ropes.

"Enough with the old junk, Aaron," Owen called out at one point. "Teach him to steer!" Everyone on board, weary of their bones being bounced around when Henry was at the wheel, laughed loudly.

Owen did his best to get along with Thacher. It was easier than he expected. The boy's disposition seemed to brighten with each day he spent in the sun and salt air instead of retrieving barrels and stowing supplies in the now all but forgotten hold. And as the young crew avoided the dark world below the deck, a new order was established above it.

Owen continued to give most of the orders, when they were needed, but it was mostly clear what needed doing. Much of it was long established aboard the ship and seemed as inevitable as the sunrise. Adjusting the sails as the wind changed, taking your trick at the helm . . .

But some things did change. First names took the place of barked titles. Aaron was no longer "You, powder monkey." He was simply Aaron. The others no longer had "boy" affixed to the front of their names to bring them low. "Boy Owen" was simply "Owen." They were all equal in their youth now. And they no longer had their ears twisted or arms tugged by officers unsatisfied with their work.

The biggest change, of course, was that two of the ship's boys were now known to be ship's girls. Owen did his best to ignore the fact. It was a truth widely acknowledged on sailing ships that you could hand, reef, and steer, or you could not. He had seen how the distinctions of race, country, and class that so bedeviled men on land could fall away after a few weeks at sea, outweighed by competence, reliability, and skill. Aaron himself, he'd heard, was half Pequot.

So why should gender prove any trickier? He no longer believed that females were bad luck on a ship. The Spanish sisters were undeniable assets, and he increasingly relied on Emma, in particular.

Still, now that their tightly wrapped Spanish style had come undone, it seemed amazing to him that he had ever thought them to be boys. He couldn't deny that it changed things somewhat. The two had always conversed in Spanish now and then, sometimes whispered and sometimes spoken. The understanding was always that they were sharing secrets, talking among themselves. Owen just didn't remember ever being so interested in what those secrets might be.

Especially Emma. What was she saying? Did she think he was a good sailor? Did she think of him at all? He tried to shake these thoughts from his head as soon as they arrived. But like a flock of starlings, they would come home to roost whenever he had time for idle thoughts.

Fortunately, there wasn't much of that. The crew was careful now to take in sail when the wind picked up and to let it back out when it dwindled. It seemed they were always either up in the rigging or coming down from it. By the third day, Owen noted, Henry was coming up with them. *Still not nearly keeping up*, he noted, but sometimes small steps were in order. And that was especially true when those steps took place seventy feet above a pitching deck.

All in all, it was easy to get along when things were going well. And even with a skeleton crew—and a few cut corners—the work was still manageable in fair weather.

But at the end of that fourth day, they ran out of supplies above deck. With no rain since the last quick squall, the scuttle-butt was nearly dry. The barrel of salt pork was mostly gone—and the sun had not been kind to what remained. The biscuits, meanwhile, had been done in by covert nibbling.

"It was going to run out sooner or later," said Maria, by all accounts the primary biscuit burglar.

"True," said Owen. He knew the same could be said of the good weather and goodwill, but he was in no hurry to speed the process along with needless confrontation. "But we will need to go below again, regardless. Nor will this be the last time."

The others muttered their assent as Owen looked up into the late-day sky and then down at the grate at his feet. He stared into the gloom below. *Was there really something down there?* he thought for the hundredth time. *And could that truly be why the mutineers had abandoned ship?* He considered it, and then, in words that would haunt him to the end, he thought, *How bad could it truly be?*

He looked around at the others. He knew they were thinking much the same. The thought of ordering two people below again seemed cruel, especially considering the amiable new order on board. He honestly wasn't even sure he could find two people who would obey.

"Perhaps we should all go?" he said.

The others looked around at each other, noncommittal. He searched his mind for something to sweeten the pot, to make the trip seem a bit less scary. He began to open his mouth before he really knew what he was going to say, and what came out surprised even him.

"I know where there's a gun."

CHAPTER 14

BETTER ARM OURSELVES

"Should I stay at the wheel?" asked Aaron hopefully.

Henry watched as Owen looked up at the sails and then straight ahead. He was pretty sure he even knew what Owen was looking at: light winds and small waves. He'd begun to get a bit of a feel for life at sea. His knees no longer wobbled quite so much as he made his way across the swaying deck, and he no longer lost a portion of his meals over the rail when the seas picked up. He looked down at his arms, which had progressed from an angry red to a dark and even tan.

"No," said Owen. "We'll tie the wheel off. We'll want all hands for this."

Owen consulted the compass once more, and then they looped rope over two of the spokes of the ship's wheel, fixing it more or less on course. Henry tied one of the loops himself, a basic slipknot that Aaron had taught him the day before.

"Is this entirely safe?" he asked as Maria lobbed a loop over a spoke on the other side.

"Nothing is entirely safe," said Owen.

"That's right," said Aaron, nodding emphatically.

"But there's a device somewhere in the neighborhood of the tiller meant to give it a little play, in case the wheel gets stuck," continued Owen. He paused and added, "Or the helmsman gets shot."

And on that note, they all followed Owen back to the cabin, their last stop before heading down the hatch.

"Is it the captain's gun?" said Thacher.

"It's not, neither," said Aaron. "His gun is . . ." His voice trailed off. They all knew where that gun was: at the bottom of the sea. Henry remembered the quick crack of gunshots sounding through the cabin door.

Owen didn't answer; he just opened the freshly mended cabin door and went in. The lantern had been left burning. Owen turned it up as he passed, and the room came fully into view. Henry watched Owen's back as he squatted down and began rooting through a polished leather sea trunk. His shoulder muscles moved visibly under his shirt and vest. Compact, powerful, and hunched over to forage, he reminded Henry of a chimpanzee he'd seen once. *Pan troglodytes*, he thought, remembering the creature's scientific name. *Owen troglodytes*.

Owen grunted, completing the effect, and then stood up. He brought a rectangular wooden box over to the table, below the hanging lantern.

"Oooh," said Thacher as he saw the polished wood and silver clasps of the box.

Owen pressed a button on the front with his thumbs and the clasps popped open: *tik-tik*.

"It's *ceremonial*," said Owen, deploying the word with both pride and care. "He got it for rescuing some shipwrecked Frenchman or other, but I never saw him use it—or even carry it."

The room fell silent, and Henry craned his neck for a better look. The pistol was pressed into an indentation in the velvet lining of the case, formed to hold it snugly. The wood of the gun was dark and smooth, and the metal was bright and decorated with ornate etchings. Below its barrel, a small flask of gunpowder and eight polished lead balls—or were they silver?—had their own little homes in the velvet.

Henry took half a step back as Owen gingerly pried the pistol from its case. Was it loaded?

Owen wrapped his hand around the pistol's grip, his finger resting lightly alongside the trigger guard. The gun's intricate etchings caught the light as Owen pointed it at a blank stretch of wall. Henry saw a little ship riding waves of fine metal lines along the barrel, all sails set. He didn't know much about guns, but he knew this was what they called a flintlock. He admired it from a purely scientific perspective. He saw the black wedge of flint in the hammer. When the trigger was pulled, he knew, the hammer would fall, striking the metal plate and creating a spark. That would ignite the gunpowder in the barrel and send the lead ball flying forward at high velocity. It was what happened after that—what happened when the lead ball hit its target—that made him a little queasy.

"The way I figure it," said Owen, "if there is something down there, we'd better arm ourselves."

Henry could hear the fresh confidence in his voice. Guns did that to men, he knew. That part made him a little queasy too. He was not the one holding the gun after all, and he figured he probably never would be. The others were less impressed, though.

"And the way I figure it," said Thacher, "if it's a ghost down there, a gun won't do one whit of good."

Owen frowned, though he couldn't quite manage to pull his eyes away from the gleaming weapon in his hand.

"He's right," said Aaron. "What more can a bullet do to Obed Macy that hasn't been done already?"

Emma crossed herself at the sound of the missing boy's name, and Henry was surprised to find himself surrounded by so much superstition. Emma and Aaron too?

"We just need a different sort of weapon," said Maria.

Henry looked at her. Had they all lost their minds? Was it really just he and Owen who were still concerned with the real physical world around them?

Emma was nodding fiercely. "We need the good book," she said.

"I have this," said Owen, lowering the pistol and pulling a small silver cross from under his shirt by its leather cord.

Incredible, thought Henry. *I have lost the chimp too.*

Emma looked skeptical. "That is something," she said. "But where is the captain's Bible?"

Owen pointed the gun at the desk in the corner, looking for a moment as if he meant to execute the thing. "Top drawer," he said.

Emma glared at Owen until he lowered the gun, and then she walked over to the desk.

Henry waited for her to return to the huddled group before posing a theory of his own. "What if it's a mutineer down there?" he said. "How can we be certain they all left the ship?"

"It's true," said Aaron, willing to consider any possible danger. "It *could* be a mutineer. Could be he was hurt in the fight."

"A wounded animal," said Owen, considering it. "Dangerous . . ."

Henry looked around at the others. They seemed to be at least entertaining the thought. He honestly wasn't sure if he believed it himself, but he was glad to have restored a little rationality to the discussion. A wounded mutineer stumbling around between decks seemed like a nice middle ground: neither monster nor ghost.

"Well, if it is," said Owen, "then we will need the gun after all." He lifted its gleaming barrel toward the light.

"And they will need the Bible," said Emma, lifting its worn leather cover up as well. "For they have sinned."

The little group looked around at each other, one last moment of hesitation.

"So we are in agreement, then," said Owen. "We have the right weaponry."

The others nodded.

"But you should not have all of them," said Thacher.

Owen looked down at the gun, but that's not what Thacher wanted. "Give me the cross," he said, casting a subtle vote as to what he believed lurked below deck.

Owen lifted it from around his neck. "Be careful with this," he said, handing it over. "It was my mother's."

"Carefulness," said Thacher, slipping it around his neck, "is why I want it."

The final preparations were made. Owen poured gunpowder from the little flask down the gullet of the gun, then rolled a ball in after it, and packed it all in tightly. Then Maria took the lantern down from above the table. "Good idea," said her sister. "They don't seem to last long down below."

And with that, the little crew filed out of the cabin and toward the aft hatch. Maria was first with the lantern, Owen was next with the gun, and Emma and Thacher were next with their preferred forms of protection. Henry hung back slightly, lost in thought, which gave him a nice view of Aaron swiping one of the knives from the silverware drawer.

"I want a weapon too," he whispered once he realized he'd been seen.

"What are you going to do?" said Henry. "Butter it?"

"Better than nothing," said Aaron, slipping the dull blade beneath his ragged belt.

But Henry barely heard him. He was playing his own words over. *I said "it,"* he thought. *Not "him," but "it."* Without even meaning to, he'd cast his own subtle vote as to what lurked below.

Once again he admonished himself with three familiar words: *Be a scientist.*

But these were hard conditions for rational thought. The sky was dim above them but not yet dark. It was streaked with violet and hung with a sickle moon. But Henry knew these would provide cold comfort below, where such weak light wouldn't penetrate.

The stories played in his head—ghosts, monsters, mutineers— and so did the memories. Shadows at the edge of his vision; crashing noises, getting closer; a sickly sweet smell filling his nose.

As he grasped the rungs of the ladder and began his descent, it was the last of these that he found himself contemplating. He knew that smell, or at least that *type* of smell. It wasn't floral, though it was sweet enough to be. It was *fungal*. It was the subtle undertone of yeast—every bread lover's favorite fungus—that gave it away. He had, in fact, encountered several varieties of funguses that smelled both sweet and yeasty, and that was back in boring old Boston.

He could only imagine what wondrous varieties these tropical climates might hold. That had been the whole point of this expedition. The Amazon jungle was the ideal environment for growing all manner of things: flowers, trees, molds, fungi . . . It was the lure of all these teeming and exotic—and, above all, undiscovered—species that had cost his employer his life. And as he thought of Dr. Wetherby—of all he had taught him, and the tragic fate that had befallen the great botanist in that jungle—Henry understood something very clearly.

There *were* ghosts on this ship, as sure and real as the well-worn wood below his feet, but those ghosts weren't lurking somewhere down in the darkness. They were living in the minds of the survivors. The cook who had taught Aaron a bit of his craft, or the old salt who had taught him the knots he was now teaching Henry. The captain Owen still revered. The countless conversations between now-dead sailors that had helped shape the Spanish sisters' English. The authors of all the little slights and abuses that had left Thacher so hardened and scarred.

Maria called up from the bottom of the ladder, interrupting Henry's musing. "Shattered!" she said. "Smashed all to pieces."

It took Henry a moment to realize she was talking about the lantern—the new lantern they'd just hung there a handful of fair-weather days earlier. Something *was* breaking them intentionally.

He swallowed hard and descended into darkness.

CHAPTER 15

TURNED BACK

They stood in a little cluster at the bottom of the ladder. There was no pool of sunlight there this time. The only light came from Maria's lantern.

"Hold on tight to that lamp," said Emma. "Something down here doesn't seem to like them much."

"Someone," corrected Thacher.

Henry looked behind them and saw his own shadow stretching out into darkness. He looked back at the lantern. It didn't illuminate their surroundings as much as it illuminated *them*. *Come and get us*, it seemed to say.

"Let's move," said Owen, pointing his pistol straight down the passageway and into darkness. Henry noticed that the barrel was wobbling slightly, causing the lamplight reflecting off its polished surface to glitter and dance. *Is his hand shaking?*

They pressed forward, stepping over the busted lanterns one by one. Their little circle of light moved with them, exposing another foot of the dark passageway with each step. Henry could feel water under his feet and hear the wet slaps of the others' steps. It hadn't been this bad the last time he'd come down.

"There's more water," he whispered.

Owen stopped and looked down. He nodded grimly, pointing the gun at the wall beside them. "Aye," he said. "There are always little leaks, gaps in the hull, between the boards. The ship is long overdue for some tar and oakum to plug the gaps. She's never been a dry vessel."

The thought sent another chill up Henry's spine. But just imagine being sent down here with a bucket of tar and some bits of old rope, hunting every dark corner for gaps in the wooden planks of the hull.

"Some of it will work its way down into the bilge, and we can get it with the chain pump," said Aaron.

"Aye, we'll reach port long before we sink from small leaks," said Thacher.

Owen refused to take his eyes off the passage ahead of them, but Henry saw his shoulders stiffen at the suggestion. Even he knew that they were letting most of the day-to-day maintenance of the ship slide now. There was only so much six of them could do, especially when half their number seemed to be up in the rigging at any given time, and one always at the wheel. And that was above deck. *What else are we neglecting below?*

He now understood the complex calculus of their decision: Untended and without its carpenter, the ship was falling apart a little bit each day. It came down to how many days that would take, and whether they could reach port before then.

As they stood motionless just a few paces into their journey, he felt the captainless ship jostling along over the waves now, sending little shocks up through the soles of his cold, wet feet. He knew—not out of any knowledge of boats but just based on pure physics—that every jolt would make those little leaks a bit bigger.

Shhhuck shhhhuck. Owen peeled his feet from the wet wood and began walking again. *Splap splap.*

The huddled group reached the edge of the crew's quarters. Henry heard a few gasps and squinted into the gloom, struggling to see what the others saw. There was a grating directly overhead, but it revealed nothing but little squares of the purple sky above. Thacher leaned closer, shouldering past Henry. "What the devil?" he said.

Owen nudged Maria a bit farther out into the space, and the group took a few hesitant steps. The lamplight revealed the extent of the wreckage. Sea trunks had been torn open, their lids hanging loosely or ripped off completely on the floor nearby. A pillow had been shredded, leaving wet feathers plastered to the floor and even the hull alongside. A cloth hammock lay in tatters.

"What could have . . ." began Emma before pausing and changing her question mid-sentence. "What is *that smell*?"

Henry closed his mouth and took a deep whiff through his nose. The wet funk of the crew's quarters was immediately overpowered by an air of sweet decay.

"It's *him*!" said Thacher, raising the borrowed cross up and holding it out in front of him.

"Hold your ground," growled Owen. His voice sounded impressively brave to Henry, until he noticed the barrel of the pistol flopping around like a fish on a dock. "We still need those supplies."

But the others were already starting to step back, leaving Owen alone and exposed in the ravaged quarters. Even the light was slowly retreating from him, illuminating only his back now. "We can get them tomorrow," said Aaron, his voice breaking into a high squeak halfway through the last word.

"Do you suppose it will be any better then?" said Owen, his head still forward, as if talking to the darkness.

Henry filled his nostrils again, only halfway this time, trying to pull the odor apart slowly. Trying to match it with the scientific specimens he'd encountered back in Boston and on his travels with the doctor: oddly colored mushrooms, little sprays of fuzz . . .

"Perhaps not," said Thacher, "but it will be *brighter*."

Owen suddenly seemed to recognize that all the voices were coming from behind him and that he was standing at the very edge of the light. He swung around, his eyes wide, and his gun suddenly pointed at the rest of the group.

For a moment, Henry honestly thought he might shoot one of them for having abandoned him. Instead, he cocked his head slightly, in that doglike way of his, and said, "True . . ."

As he did, Henry saw something shift in the darkness behind him. What it was he could not say: just a pale circle flashing across the murk and a quick glitter of something catching the light. Something dark but shiny—or perhaps dark but wet. As it flashed across his vision, strange sounds rose to accompany it.

Henry heard a quick series of wet scratches, as if a dull blade was being dragged through wet wood, and then *breahhkrehka brehkah* . . .

It was a breathy rasp unlike anything he had heard before. It was utterly alien but also, somehow, vaguely human.

"RUN!" called Emma. "Do not turn around, cabin boy. Just run!"

Owen's eyes, which had grown wider still at the sound, narrowed now. He bolted forward. He quickly caught up with the rest of the group, and they all stampeded down the passage together.

"AAH!" screamed Maria as they neared the ladder.

"What is it?" gulped Owen. "Are you struck?"

"No," she said, stopping short at the base of the ladder. "I stepped on one of the broken lanterns. Cut my foot."

She held the lamp steady as the others climbed toward the square of purple sky above.

Henry looked down from his spot in the chain of climbers. He saw Owen wave her up. "Go!" he said, pointing his wobbling pistol straight down the passage.

Maria nodded and began to climb, holding the lantern above her and leaving the terrified cabin boy and a trail of bloody footprints behind her.

Henry climbed fast, making way for those behind him. When he reached the top, he tumbled onto the deck. Breathing hard, he stared back at the hatch. Emma emerged, and then her sister.

"Owen . . ." Henry breathed.

But no sooner had he said his name than the boy emerged, popping like a jack-in-the-box from the open hatch. "What?" he said.

Henry shook his head. *Nothing*, he thought. *Just glad to see you.*

They battened down the hatches and then dropped heavy coils of rope on top. For an hour or so, they busied themselves with breathless recountings of their trip below and wild speculation as to what it was they hadn't quite seen.

"Not a ghost, I think," said Owen.

"Not a normal one, anyway," admitted Thacher.

Henry looked at him in the moonlight. *What exactly was a normal ghost?*

But soon their excitement drained and they grew tired.

Watches were set. It was Owen's crew's turn to sleep first. He handed the pistol to Emma—a single shot still primed within its barrel—as he slunk wearily toward the cabin.

Each in their turn, the crew members slept fitfully, on empty stomachs and with minds full of nightmares. Henry hadn't eaten since breakfast—and that had only been a spoonful of molasses and some last crumbs of sea bread. The hunger gnawed at him—*Who would have thought one could miss old salt pork so much?*—but the thirst was worse. The day had been hot and bright.

He smacked his dry mouth and it made a thick, gluey sound. He knew that they would have to go below again in the morning. They would have to confront some still faceless horror. They would have to risk the possibility of death below deck or endure the certainty of starvation above.

But maybe they could hold off until it rained again?

Maybe they could catch some food from the sea?

They were nice thoughts, if impractical, and the moment's respite allowed him to drift off to sleep.

He woke to sore muscles and rosy red light filtering in through the windows of the cabin. The dawn had arrived in purples and blues for the last few days, and he much preferred this new color. Sensing motion in the hammock beside him, he whispered, "It is quite pretty."

"It is not," said Maria sleepily. "It means there's foul weather on the way."

"Oh," said Henry, ignoring the danger as best he could and thinking only of the rainwater.

The door to the cabin swung open, and Owen stuck his head in. "Everyone up!" he called.

The night watch was over, and once again, all hands were needed on deck.

The Spanish sisters yawned in near perfect unison and tumbled out of their hammocks onto the floor. Reluctantly, Henry climbed out of his hammock to join them.

A new day had begun, with a fresh storm looming above and a mysterious danger lurking below. As Henry stepped out onto the quarterdeck and squinted up into the crimson dawn, he wondered quite seriously if this day might, in fact, be their last.

CHAPTER 16

THE FACE OF HORROR

Emma had gladly handed the gun back to Owen at the end of her watch, but now she eyed it jealously as the group made its way back toward the hatch once again. She watched the pistol bobbing loosely in Owen's right hand. She remembered that weight: cold and reassuring. She looked down at the large carving knife in her hand. It was neither quite as heavy as the pistol nor nearly as comforting. *What do I think we're fighting here?* she thought. *A cooked turkey?*

Owen stuck the pistol in his belt and knelt down to clear off the hatch cover.

"Anyone else get the sinking feeling we've been here before?" said Thacher.

When no one answered, he went on: "What makes us think this time will be any different?"

"It's light now," said Owen. "Remember?"

He grunted as he shoved the heavy coil of rope aside and then added, "We will be able to see more clearly."

Emma looked at him: *So literal.*

Thacher looked at him too. "Do you imagine that an improvement?"

"I would rather go to my grave never getting a closer look at that thing," said Aaron.

Owen, already removing the wooden battens, looked up. "Be careful what you wish for," he said.

Emma smiled. *Not so literal after all.* She knelt down to help him remove the hatch cover.

A few moments later, they stood peering into the opening. Emma looked down at the square of morning sunlight at the bottom. Her sister's bloody footprints were still visible on the rungs of the ladder. She glanced back at Maria, who was standing at the helm. The seas were too high to tie the wheel today, and Maria's injured foot made her the obvious choice to take it. Emma looked at the scrap of cloth wrapped around her sister's foot: dark red, edging toward brown. At least the bleeding had stopped.

Emma felt a sudden tenderness for her sister, who had come so far with her and been through so much. Maria had been right about their "Spanish style." The others didn't seem to care much that they were girls. There'd been some slights, certainly, and it was awkward when Emma looked up and caught Owen looking back. But overall, it was clear: They all had bigger things to think about these days.

Maria took a hand from the wheel and gave her sister a small wave. "*Ten cuidado*," she mouthed. *Be careful*. Emma nodded and turned back to the hatch. She was glad at least one of them was safe.

"Who goes first?" said Thacher. He turned to Henry. "You have the lantern."

"Plenty of sunlight at the bottom," Henry protested.

"I'll go," said Owen. "I have the gun."

No one argued. Owen took a deep breath, swung around, and headed straight down the ladder. Emma had expected a little more time. "Wait," she mumbled, but he would not.

"If I wait, I won't do it," he said, disappearing below deck.

The others fell in line behind him. First Henry with the lantern, then Thacher with a wicked-looking gaff hook, then Emma with her knife, and Aaron directly after her with a blade of his own. There was no Bible among them this time. Whatever they'd seen and heard the last time, it was a living thing.

"Perhaps a bear?" Aaron had said the night before.

"A bear? Between decks?" Owen had scoffed.

"Actually, bears are good swimmers," Henry had added.

Not helpful, thought Emma, but she didn't believe for a second that it was a bear. She could still hear its horrible breathy rasp. There was something obscene about it, unholy. *Bears at least have the decency to roar*, she thought. She gripped her knife tight and felt the glaze of sweat between her palm and its wooden handle.

She reached the bottom and joined the others, huddled together in the patch of sunlight, standing in perhaps a quarter inch of seawater. She stepped aside to make room for Aaron. They all stood close together, their various weapons and trembling hands posing almost as much danger to each other as anything awaiting them.

"Maybe, we should make noise," said Emma. "It is what you do if you think there are bears in the woods. You make noise to scare them off."

The looks she got from the others told her that none of them truly believed it was a bear. "I *know* it's not a bear," she clarified. "But maybe we should treat it like one. Monsters might get scared too."

Owen looked down the hallway. Emma followed his eyes. The light from the gratings filed down in hazy beams. The gaps in between were dim but not dark. "We are not going to sneak up on it now anyhow," he said.

"All animals can be startled," said Henry. "Even the lions of Africa."

Aaron looked at him. "What's a lion?"

"It is like a bear and a cat in one."

"I hope it ain't one of those," said Aaron very seriously.

"Lord," said Thacher, "is there nothing you aren't afraid of?"

Owen ignored the chatter. Emma could see that he was thinking. His pistol was pointed down the passageway but his eyes were far off. Suddenly, he blinked and looked up. "Yes," he said loudly. "We will move fast. Grab food and water. We will raise the dickens the whole way, shouting and stomping. We will scare off this thing, be it bear or man or . . ." He turned to Henry.

"Lion?" said Henry.

"Aye," said Owen. "Be it that either."

"And what if it we don't scare it off?" said Aaron.

"Then we shall shoot it and stab it until it wishes we had!"

"The devil doesn't scare so easily," muttered Thacher, and Emma could see that he was still wearing Owen's silver cross. "Nor does he bleed."

She would not let this gloomy boy darken their intrepid mood. "Hurrah!" she said, a rousing vote for her own plan.

"Hurrah for food and water!" said Aaron.

"I'll cheer to that," said Henry.

They looked to Thacher, who raised his gaff hook in weak solidarity.

"Let's go!" boomed Owen, leading the charge.

And with that, they stormed the between deck. Weapons up and voices raised, they bashed and stomped their way down the passage and to the galley. Emma's heart pounded with heavy, fast thumps that she could feel in her head. But nothing rose to stop them.

Emma smiled as they reached the galley, and Owen swung open the door with the barrel of his pistol. But a new problem arose immediately. They couldn't haul the food and hold their weapons at the same time.

"Grab what you can," said Owen, pulling back the hammer of the pistol. "I will cover you."

Emma and Thacher squatted down to lift a heavy barrel of water, their weapons piled on top. Emma was sure the gaff hook would cost her an eye before she saw the sun again. Aaron and Henry wrestled with a barrel of salted meat.

"Not more pork," said Thacher. "I am sick of pork. Get that one there, the beef."

Aaron and Henry pivoted to the next barrel. "I can balance either the lantern upon it or some of these biscuits," said Henry.

"Give me the lamp," said Owen, reaching over with his free hand, his gun still trained on the open door. "Take the sea bread."

"Come on, come on," said Emma as Henry stacked two large tins of biscuits on the top of the barrel, then knelt down to lift it all.

"Heave, you dogs!" said Owen, and they did.

Owen went out the door first, his pistol held at arm's length. Henry and Aaron followed, squatting on either side of the barrel and taking small sideways steps. They turned to fit out the door and then disappeared. Emma and Thacher were last.

They squeezed through the galley door and immediately ran into Henry's back. As Emma filled her lungs to shout at him, she caught the scent that had stopped him. It was a smell of sweet rot. *Oh no.*

"Go! Go!" said Owen, swinging around to cover their backs.

The other four shuffled down the passageway as fast as their heavy loads and straining limbs would allow. Emma's eyes burned but she refused to blink. She swung her head all around as the light from above faded in and out. But it was her ears that warned her first.

It made her think of an anchor dragging across a rocky sea bottom: a wet, raking sound. The little supply line stopped cold.

"OWEN!" she called. "Up here!"

She heard his quick footsteps slapping past her across the wet floorboards. And then she heard something else.

Shyehck sheck shhhyehhk . . .

That horrible breathy rasp again. She glanced down at her carving knife, its handle pinned under her chin, its sharp metal blade just beyond. Should she drop the barrel to wield the knife?

She looked up again, and there, illuminated by the checkerboard light from the grating, was the very face of horror. She dropped the barrel a split second before Thacher did, causing it to tip her way. Thacher's gaff hook skittered across the lid, nicked her cheek, and fell to the wet floor. The sound of its metal clatter was entirely drowned out, however, by that of her scream.

The face of horror, it turned out, was a familiar one. It stared down at her now, glazed with clear slime, its bloodshot eyes unblinking.

CHAPTER 17

NO TURNING BACK

Emma straightened up and took a step back. She stared at this thing, trying to make sense of what she was seeing. Obed Macy's face stared back at her. It looked glazed and slick, and she could see a heavy glob of some clear, thick substance drooping from his chin, stretching thinner, preparing to fall.

But it wasn't Obed Macy. The face of the missing hold rat stared out at them from what looked like a living helmet. It was dark red, almost black, larger than his head had been and entirely hairless. Instead of the greasy brown hair she remembered, two thin black stalks sprouted from the line of raw skin where the strange red sheathing met what had once been his forehead. The stalks waved like tall grass in a light breeze. *Alive*, Emma realized, feeling a sudden urge to vomit.

She swallowed down the bile and looked at the creature in its entirety. If the face had been at least somewhat familiar, the body below it was like nothing she'd ever seen. It was covered with the same thick red sheathing, but now she could see that it came in sections, large plates that met and sometimes overlapped. *Like a bug*, she thought. *Like an enormous bug*. And every one of those plated sections was glazed and wet.

The creature stood on two legs. They were about the length Obed's had been, but they were now covered in their living armor. She saw large, hooked barbs sprouting from the feet, as if this creature was standing on giant thorns. It had two more limbs where Obed's arms had been; they were thinner than the legs, but otherwise identical. Emma took in the barbs there with a gasp and saw them for what they were: weapons.

In between the arms and legs was another set of segmented limbs: half the size of the others, the appendages hanging from the creature's sides, twitching with odd little spasms and dripping the same slime that glazed Obed's face. *Half-formed*, she realized. *Incomplete*.

She had taken in all of this instantly, the way she could take in the ship, the sky above, and the sea beyond in a single flash of lightning. But the frozen moment passed, and the world came crashing back.

"Dear L-Lord above," stammered Thacher from across the barrel. "It is Obed Macy!"

"It is not him," called Owen. "It cannot be."

Emma said nothing, but she knew that, somehow, they were both right.

For a few seconds, the creature just stood there in the center of the passage, its barbed arms spread wide to form a fearsome barrier, its thin antennas swaying. Emma's brain reeled. The sight was clear and vivid but it seemed impossible. The real and the fantastic collided like waves breaking against a rocky cliff.

And then the creature opened its mouth. Emma saw Obed Macy's lips part beneath the thin layer of slime. A thick tongue flicked out into the light, fuzzy and fetid and white, as if made of old milk and soft cloth.

Hehhhhhhhhhhhh, it hissed, and with the hiss came an overwhelming scent of sweet decay. Emma slapped her hand over her mouth and nose.

"Back to the forward hatch!" called Aaron, sounding the retreat.

Emma turned to look back up the passage, and as she did, she saw Henry. He hadn't said a word this whole time, and now she saw why. His mouth hung open in horror and awe, but it was his eyes that struck her most. A beam of light fell squarely on them from above and she read his expression. Fear, yes, but also recognition. He wore the look of a boy having a sudden realization. *Has he seen something like this before?* she wondered. *How is that even possible?*

"We cannot!" shouted Owen. "That hatch is still covered."

There would be no going back, and as if understanding that, the creature came for them. It lurched forward, dragging its barbed feet heavily across the wet wood, producing an all-too-familiar dragging sound. Emma whipped her head back around in time to see a spasm shoot through the creature's armored body. All six of its limbs twitched, knocking it slightly off balance as it took its next step.

But still it shambled forward.

Its murderous, barbed arms twitched and swayed in the air just a few yards away as she and the others reluctantly gave ground, backing away from the only exit and into the darkness. There was something vaguely familiar about the clumsy way it was moving, but Emma had no time to figure out what it was. Instead, she sucked in just enough sickly sweet air to fill her lungs. She dropped her hand from her mouth and shouted, "Shoot it, Owen!"

And it was that word, not consciously chosen—"it"—that told her what she truly felt. Whatever they were looking at, she was sure *it* was no longer Obed Macy.

But then something happened to cast that gut-level conviction into doubt.

Beside her, Owen raised his gun. His shaking hand rose to the level of the thing's face.

The creature stopped cold. Its unblinking eyes opened wider, staring at the pistol. She recognized the expression immediately because she'd seen it just seconds earlier, albeit on a different face. It was fear mixed with recognition. Fear of the gun . . . *Obed?* she thought. *Is he still in there?*

The gun was loaded, cocked, and leveled. The tug of Owen's finger was all that remained.

Emma watched as the creature, or Obed, or—she wasn't even sure anymore, but she watched as their attacker began to slowly shamble backward. The heavy feet dragged as the other four limbs twitched and swayed.

"It moves like old Wrickitts," said Aaron in a horrified whisper.

Yes, that's it, she thought. *That's what is familiar.* But she wasn't the only one who seemed to recognize the name.

No sooner was it uttered than the creature ceased its retreat. Its eyes narrowed, its lips flattened, and it bared its boy's teeth as it hissed once again. It lurched forward, faster this time.

Emma heard a small, crisp click from directly beside her head as Owen pulled the trigger.

Instantly, her world lit up with a fiery light and filled with a deafening bang. She reeled away too late. Stunned by the explosion so close to her head, she could do little more than stumble blindly back from the thing's advance.

She felt something clamp down on her shoulder and pushed it away in horror. But it was no slime-sheathed claw. It was a warm hand. She blinked her eyes open, and behind the swirling stars she saw Owen.

"It's gone," he said. "At least, I think so."

She stood up, her eyes searching the passageway. She

saw nothing under the light that streamed in from the grating, and nothing in the dark expanse directly behind that.

"Did you hit him?" she said.

"Possibly," said Owen, gazing at the same empty stretch. "But he has not fallen."

"There is no time for discussion," said Thacher. "We cannot linger down here."

Owen nodded, but as Henry tried to rush past him, he stuck out an arm and stopped him cold. Henry looked over, not comprehending, the still-warm barrel of the pistol pressed sideways against his chest, barring his way.

"Pick up the food," said Emma, explaining it to him. She gazed into the murky dim beyond the little patch of light. "We are no longer alone upon this ship, and we must take everything we can."

CHAPTER 18

A TURN FOR THE WORSE

They carried their heavy loads up the sloping ladder and dropped them on the deck. Owen emerged, last in line, still pointing the now-empty pistol down into the darkness. Had he forgotten he'd already fired his shot, wondered Emma, or was he hoping that Obed had forgotten how to count to one somewhere along the way to becoming a monster?

"What is it?" called Maria, from her post. "What did you see?"

"A beast!" Aaron answered.

"The walking remains of Obed Macy!" added Thacher.

"Nothing good," concluded Owen.

Henry said nothing, and Emma could see his mind still working, still chewing away at the bizarre sight. *What has* he *seen?* she wondered. *Does he alone know?* She turned to her sister and shook her head, her message somewhere between "I have no idea" and "You don't want to know."

Then she swung around to help batten down the hatch. As soon as the cover was on, they loaded it up with any heavy object within reach. Not just rope this time, but also the sturdy wooden blocks that those ropes slid through and other bits of equipment. For a moment, Emma wondered if they could drag one of the anchors over. She stared up at the heavy cables holding them to the ship, and that's when she saw the forward hatch.

"Save some of the ballast," she said, pointing at it.

They loaded that one down too. After they planted an old pot of dried tar on top, Aaron grabbed the ship's cat and plopped her down amid the clutter. "Don't let anything up, Daffy!" he instructed.

Daffodil hissed up at him and took off at a run for the captain's cabin.

"We'll have to guard it ourselves," said Owen. "That one doesn't have the claws for it." He paused, remembering what they'd just seen. "We'd need a lion."

He looked down at his pistol and followed the cat into the cabin to reload.

Thacher followed a few steps behind. At first, Emma didn't think much of it, but then it occurred to her where he might be going. She fell in line a few paces back.

Thacher took the three little steps up to the quarterdeck briskly, and a few moments later, Emma did the same, her bare feet cat-quiet on the well-worn wood. Just a few days earlier it would have been unthinkable for a ship's boy—much less a ship's girl—to set foot on this rarefied terrain without permission. Now they did it with barely a second thought.

Thacher stopped short alongside the wheel. Emma nodded grimly behind him. She'd been right.

"I'll take over," Thacher told Maria. "Your trick's up by now."

Maria shifted her gaze from the ocean ahead to the boy beside her. Then she looked over his shoulder at her sister. Thacher followed her gaze and turned. He jumped slightly, his nerves worn as thin as everyone else's. "What are you doing here?" he said.

"It's not your turn," said Emma flatly. "You're not even on the same watch."

"What's it to you?" he said, already turning away and stepping back toward the wheel. "Some time at the helm will calm my nerves is all."

But is *that all?* Emma wondered.

Thacher put a hand on the wheel, grabbing one of the spokes and swinging around by it. He seemed willing to shoulder Maria out of the way, but before he could, she released the wheel and stepped aside.

"Fine with me," she said. Looking straight into Emma's eyes she added, "We need to talk anyway. I want to know what happened down there—I heard the gunshot."

Emma took one more look at Thacher, standing tall and looking diligent enough at the wheel. Then she looked back at her sister. "Fine," she said. "But you will not like it."

The sisters turned and headed forward, leaning in and

talking low. Emma struggled to find the words—in English, Spanish, or anything else that might spring to mind—to describe the horror she'd seen beneath that grating. Maria refused to believe what she had heard, interrupting with "Are you sure?" and "No!" and "It is very hard to see clearly down there."

As they descended from the quarterdeck, the cabin door slapped open behind them and the shouting started. "What are you doing?" bellowed Owen. "Have you lost your senses?"

"On the contrary," Thacher called back, "I have found them."

Emma glanced down at his hands and saw them pulling hard to the left. A moment later, the big ship answered, pitching over to its side as its course changed. *That rat!* she thought. She knew he'd been up to something.

Owen stepped forward but Thacher refused to even look in his direction. He was steering hard left: straight toward the nearest land, straight toward Central America. She knew, because she had briefly considered doing the same thing.

"I am taking her straight to shore," yelled Thacher. "I care not where!"

"You will not!" growled Owen.

Suddenly, the two boys were side by side, and there were four hands on the wheel instead of two.

"Let him do it!" called Aaron.

She turned to see the others gathered beside her on the lip of the quarterdeck, watching the wrestling match for control of the wheel. Emma's eyes flicked down toward the reloaded pistol, stuck into Owen's belt. It was all so familiar: the anger and shouting and the heavy tang of possible violence. A word floated into her mind, but she refused to say it, or even think it.

Then another thought occurred to her. She looked up into the canvas. The wind was stronger now. She spun and looked up toward the bowsprit. "The sails!" she shouted.

A sailing ship was guided as much with its sails as its wheel. You couldn't just make hard turns willy-nilly, without making the corresponding changes to the sails. She searched the eyes of those around her. Who would help her? She looked back toward the wheel, her eyes pleading for some sort of order.

What she saw there calmed her nerves, at least for a moment. Bigger and stronger, Owen simply overpowered Thacher for control of the wheel. Once the smaller boy's hands were free of the spokes, Owen shouldered him aside. Thacher hesitated and then stepped clear.

The tension faded and Emma exhaled. It had been a mutinous moment, or nearly so, but it had passed. Thacher had no stomach for a losing battle.

Slowly and steadily, with his eyes on the horizon, Owen began to steer the ship back to starboard. "The sails are in order," he said. "Though we won't be needing those royals in this wind."

He peeled his eyes from the sails and looked down at the assembled crew. "We have seen a horrible thing this day, but it either ran from this gun or fell from its blast. Perhaps it lies dead already."

It, thought Emma. *If I had pulled that trigger, I wouldn't say his name either.* She remembered the scene and tried to reconcile Owen's boastful tone now with his shaking hand then.

"Either way," he continued, "I will have no more talk of this ridiculous business. The nearest port?" He repeated the phrase, spitting it out with disdain: "*The nearest port?* Do you have any idea where we are in the world?"

He stared at Aaron and then shot a look back at Thacher. "These are wild ports, full of slavers and pirates. Wild ports, and foreign. Six children alone? The ship would be sold out from under us in a moment. And then we would be sold, in turn. Sold, or worse."

And here his eyes found Emma and her sister. It was a fierce look, and she felt a shudder run through her. He opened his mouth as if to say something more. Emma feared what it might be. What dire threat or prediction? Instead, Owen closed his mouth and shook his head.

"What of the government of, well, of wherever it is we land?" said Henry, his voice a peep.

Owen seemed not to hear him, or at least did not acknowledge him. Emma answered instead. "Who do you think would take the ship?"

Henry gazed back at her, shocked. For a moment she envied

him. How soft had his upbringing been that he had no idea how the world worked out here, in the wide seas beyond New York or Boston or wherever this frail boy had been hatched.

But it was a harmless question, and as Henry stood beside her, still considering the implications of her words, she leaned in to ask him one with a bit more bite.

"You know what that was down there, don't you?" she said into the whipping wind. "I saw it . . . in your eyes."

Henry looked over at her, and she could see now that those same eyes were watering. She hoped it was from the stiff salt breeze.

He met her gaze. "It was . . ." he began, before pausing to find the right word. And despite his strange frailty—or maybe because of it—she had no doubt he would choose the right one. "It was a *transformation*," he said.

She nodded. The word was almost the same in Spanish: *transformación*.

He continued. "Two separate species are somehow—"

"Somehow what?" interrupted Maria. "What are you two talking about?" She was leaning in and whispering too. Secrets, Emma knew, were among her sister's favorite things. *Even if she's not so great at keeping them.*

"Stow that grub!" Owen shouted up from the wheel, shattering the quiet shared moment. "We've rough seas ahead, and we don't want to lose any of it overboard."

The sky was darkening behind the ship, and the wind was picking up again. Whatever was coming, it would be no passing squall this time.

"We'll need to take in some sail," Emma called back as the first drops of rain began to fall. She heard them on the deck and felt them in her matted hair.

Owen, Thacher, and the rest of the crew turned to look at the ominous sky, each one of them with a weather eye, trying to gauge how much time they had before the storm struck. There was nothing like foul weather to bring a crew together.

As they gazed skyward, a huge gust of wind struck the ship from the southeast, once again well in advance of the looming clouds. The sails stretched fore and aft, the timber groaned, and the ship was knocked nearly on its side.

"It crept up on us!" called Aaron. "Sneaky devil!"

Emma fell to one knee to keep her balance. Henry, with the weakest sea legs, hit the deck beside her, rolling like a tumbleweed toward the rail. She wondered, with that strange dreaminess that sometimes accompanies mortal danger, if that was the last she would see of him.

For in a world with monsters and slavers, a world where no port was truly safe, there was still no quicker or surer death than that offered by foul weather at sea.

The gust had come from out of a blue sky and vanished into a graying one. As the wind relented, the ship righted herself. But as it rolled back to something like level, the waves slapping against her hull were already growing.

"It's coming up fast!" Owen called from the wheel. "We can ride its edge, stay ahead of it!"

And for a while, it worked. The wind increased steadily, with only occasional gusts, and none like the sudden wallop that had nearly swamped them. Emma held on tight to the rail and took in the state of things. The hatches were battened down and then some, and they'd covered the gratings. The mainmast was missing its big mainsail, but the trysail was puffed out aft and the foremast was wearing plenty of canvas. The sailcloth was quickly soaked, turning a darker gray as the sky soured above them and the rain began to pore down in buckets. But wet sails hauled wind well, and if nothing else cracked or split, she thought they might just be able to stay ahead of the worst of it until the storm blew itself out or passed them by.

"We're going to make it!" she shouted through the whistling wind to her sister, just feet away. She smiled crazily at the simple thought of survival.

But her sister was not smiling back. She was looking straight ahead.

Emma whipped her head around. "Oh no," she murmured, her words eaten alive by the wind.

What she saw was the big ship sliding down the back of a long swell. "Hold on!" she yelled, and not just to her sister this time.

The bow slammed hard into the waiting sea, punching through like a spoon into soup. Emma felt her head whipped forward. A moment later, a wave of seawater flooded across the deck as the ship rose back up on the face of the next swell. But it didn't rise as high as it had before, and when it slid down the back of it, it dove even deeper. Emma watched in both horror and recognition as the long bowsprit at the front of the boat harpooned the water.

As the boat rose again, it brought with it a heavy load of seawater that rolled down the deck in a great frothy wave.

And again the boat rose up only to be driven down.

And again.

And again.

And each time, it rose up less and was driven down more.

Grasping the rail with sore, wet hands as another wave threatened to carry her away, Emma stared up at the sails once more, and this time she saw the problem. The topmost royals had already been reefed, but it wasn't enough. They were still wearing too much sail—and in the wrong places. "It's burying us!" she called back to Owen. "It's driving us under!"

But Owen was being tossed around by the wheel like a rag doll. It was all he could do to try to keep hold of the thing and keep the ship pointed forward. If they turned crossways to these seas, they would be finished.

Emma peeled one hand off the rail and grabbed her sister's arm. "This rig is all wrong," she shouted, slapping her hand back onto the rail. "Too front heavy!"

Maria's eyes grew wide as she looked up. With the mainsail stripped bare amidships, the foremast was carrying most of the sail. Now the strong storm winds were filling those forward sails and driving the bow down into the sea. And that was slowing them down, allowing the worst of the storm to catch up.

Emma was sure it would sink them. As if to confirm her fears, she heard a shout from Owen and looked back to see that he'd lost control of the wheel, which was spinning wildly to the side.

When she looked back, Maria was staring at her, shaking her head. "Don't do it! You can't lay aloft in this!"

"I have to!" she called. "I have to take in some of the sail up high!"

As the boat began to turn sideways to the swells, a huge wave smashed against the hull, spraying seawater across the deck. As the rest of the wave passed beneath the ship and the port side rose high in the air, Emma heard a sickening crack. It sounded like breaking bone but was as loud as a gunshot. Wet wood giving way.

One of the port-side cannons had broken free.

Larger ships, she knew, kept their cannons below deck, and

a loose cannon could easily sink them. But the *Polaris* was too small for that. Her cannons were kept on deck—and now one of them had broken free of its moorings. Emma watched it careen across the tilted deck. It smacked into its opposite number on the starboard side with a deafening metallic *CLACK*. Both cannons—and much of the railing around them—plunged overboard into the roiling sea.

The ship was tearing herself apart. Emma had to act now. Without so much as a glance back at her sister, she began making her way, hand over hand, along the railing.

"Don't!" called her sister, but Emma didn't look back. She looked up. The high-flying royals had already been furled on both masts, but it wasn't enough. More needed to be taken in.

She skirted past Thacher on the rail. "We need to take in the fore topgallants, at least, and reef the topsail!" she called to him.

He looked up at the heavy, wet canvas whipping and snapping in the wind. "That is no job for a girl," he shouted back.

"No job for a boy, neither!" Aaron called over from his spot, hugging the mainmast.

And sure enough, neither of them took so much as one soggy step forward. Emma shook her head in annoyance and resumed her spider-walk along the pitching rail. Thacher reached out and grabbed her arm. "If we go down," he bellowed, a maniacal smile spreading across his face, "we take that *thing* down with us!"

Not willing to take his other hand off the rail, he nodded down toward the dark space below deck. She had heard something like this before, this idea of mutual destruction as a sort of victory, and she wondered once again why it held such allure for the males of her species. She shook free of his grasp.

"We are not sinking!" she shouted. "Not if I can help it."

The boat began to swing back around, and she realized without looking back that Owen had regained control of the wheel.

"Keep 'er straight, Owen!" she called. She doubted he could hear her through all of this, but lightning flashed and she was sure he could see her as she took a deep breath and hoisted herself up into the rain-slicked ratlines of the foremast.

The wind whipped around her as she climbed, and the driving rain slammed and slapped against her skin. Many times, one foot slipped or one hand was tugged nearly free. If both happened at once, she knew she would be flung to the deck or sea below—a crushing death or a watery one.

The higher up she went, the worse it got. The wind grew harder and louder, and the motion of the ship was amplified by the lever of the mast. But what could she do? She kept climbing. The sheer familiarity of the motion calmed her some. She had always been good at this.

Soon the shrouds narrowed and she reached the topgallant yard. Without hesitating, she slid along the treacherous wooden spit, her calloused feet gripping the footrope beneath her as surely as any monkey had ever gripped a vine.

And then, the tempest swirling all about her and the lightning flashing above, she began gathering in heavy, wet canvas. At first, it was too much, but she'd learned a thing or two recently. She removed her knife from its sheath. Then she reached down, much as Owen had done, and gashed the taut canvas. The wind instantly pushed through the wounds, turning them into flapping, snapping mouths. She leaned out and all but filleted the upper reaches of the sail. And as the wind pushed through, she heard the canvas began to tear further.

A bit of the pressure relieved, she began to haul in the wounded sail, timing her tugs to the little lulls in between gusts. She tied off her gains when she could, creating what looked like belt loops in the canvas. It was a nearly superhuman feat, one girl against all that sail in the teeth of a gale. But even small bodies are capable of great strength in times of crisis. Emmanuelle Iglesias understood what needed to be done, and grabbing fistfuls of wet canvas and dodging its snapping edges, she did it. Soon, though she could not say how soon, her aching arms and bleeding hands were tying knots she knew by heart, securing the topgallant sail tight to the yard.

She was already nearly spent when she descended to the forward topsail. It was lower down and the yards a bit thicker, but the sail itself was larger and heavier. She was sure it would be impossible by herself. But this one, she would not have to battle alone. As she was climbing down, she saw her sister, her long black hair whipping wildly about her, climbing up to join her. And just a few steps behind Maria, Thacher appeared, his wiry frame hunched like a baboon, his face grim as the death he thought he was climbing toward. And behind him, Aaron too had joined their mad bid to save the ship.

It still wasn't much—four undersized sailors in a tempest— but they were used to working these sails together now. Even under these extreme conditions, they moved in unison. They held on for dear life during the worst of the dips and gusts and jolts, but a moment later they'd be hauling as one once again. At times they achieved a perilous sort of leverage by pulling as the ship climbed the steep waves, adding their own body weight to what their muscles could manage. Working as a team, they took in as much of the topsail's canvas as they dared, tied it off, and descended back to the pitching deck.

Emma looked back toward the helm, where Owen was gripping the wheel with everything he had, and then up at the canvas. *Have we taken in enough?* But already she could see that the ship's bow was riding higher, skipping over the worst of the waves rather than diving down into them.

Behind them, the stout little trysail was doing more of the work. Even without its mainsail, the mainmast was still catching plenty of wind—and in the teeth of a storm there was plenty of wind to catch. Above them, the foremast was doing its share, and no more.

Thank God, Emma thought.

Her knees felt ready to buckle and her eyes ready to close. Every last bit of her strength had been spent. But as tired as she was, she still had one more thing to do. She waited for Thacher to slink past her and then reached out and grabbed him hard by the shirt.

"If you tell me one more time what is or *is not* a job for a girl, I will do to you what I did to that topgallant," she said flatly. "Do you understand me?"

Thacher's eyes grew wide. His mouth dropped open but no words came out. Instead, he nodded slowly, once, twice, three times. On the third, Emma released his shirt and went to find someplace to sit down.

The *Polaris* and her young crew rode the edge of the storm for another two hours before the worst of it passed them by off their port side. They all but flew over the waves, making grand time. By and by, the sky lightened, and just before dusk, the sun broke through, winking at them from low on the horizon before sinking away.

CHAPTER 19

A SCIENTIFIC ENQUIRY

They spent the next few days patching the ship up as best they could. The first priority: the hatches. The heavy junk they'd layered on top had been washed away by the storm, but there was plenty of broken wood around now to nail them tight.

"And stay down there!" Aaron said after driving home the last nail in the forward hatch.

They got to work mending the topgallant sail Emma had gutted, and beyond that, they improvised. By the time they were done, the sail was patched up like a penniless giant's socks; there was stout rope where the railing had been, and there was more scrap wood covering the spots where the cannons had torn loose from the deck.

Not very handy, Henry had helped out where he could. Mostly that had involved fetching tools. He was at least well qualified for that, having taken inglorious shelter in the little toolshed for most of the storm. It was only later, after being battered by buckets and hammers, that he learned the loose cannon had missed the little shed by mere feet.

And then, of course, there were the endless turns on the

chain pump. After all that, he was as tired as any of them when he finally crawled into his hammock that night. And yet, sleep took its time finding him. It wasn't his uselessness during the storm that was bothering him. He'd gotten a bit better on board, but even the cannons hadn't been able to stay on deck during that storm.

No, what was haunting him—what was haunting all of them—was the bizarre creature they had seen below deck. Or was it *creatures*, two beings in one? On this topic, he was no longer the least qualified person on board. And now, tired but sleepless, he bent his scientific mind toward the question.

What had he seen?

A creature with the body of a large insect, the face of a boy, and the scent of something else entirely. He remembered the sickeningly sweet odor that had emanated from the creature's human mouth and the quick sight of a fuzzy white tongue glowing in the light from above. Could it be not two species in one but three?

He wanted to dismiss the idea. Surely, such a thing was impossible? But he could not dismiss his own eyes, his own nose. How many times had the old doctor told him, "You are a scientist now, and a scientist's senses are his first and best instruments"? And so he allowed himself to trust his own observations.

What might those three creatures be?

Six legs, all ending in hooked claws; an exoskeleton;

antennas . . . *An insect, certainly.* All the hallmarks of order Hymenoptera, but perhaps he could be more specific? The physical resemblance was too strong to ignore: family Formicidae . . . The ants. Without allowing time to second-guess himself, he moved on quickly. What else?

The face of a boy—a face he'd seen before, even if only in passing. *Human, plainly enough.* Or it once had been, at least. He shuddered and moved on.

This last one seemed trickier, but once again he found that he already knew the answer. He retraced familiar ground. There was much in nature that sweetened its stink: overripe fruit or rotting flowers, carnivorous pitcher plants, or nearly anything rotting away in the right damp and lightless conditions. But this was his area of expertise: He was a botanist's assistant, after all. He had stuck his nose into just about anything he had ever encountered that had even thought of blooming. In everything from botanical gardens to vegetable plots, from pristine labs to primeval forests. Some of those specimens had even fought back. He'd received several bee stings, had nasty bouts of both poison oak and ivy, and even had one Venus flytrap close quite firmly on his nose.

And so, in his expert opinion, he had his third culprit: fungus. He'd thought so the first time he smelled it, and now he felt more certain. Mold could also be a sweet little stinker. But there was the yeastiness of the scent to consider, and he had new evidence: a flash of white fuzz. He'd seen such a thing before—a pale, fibrous sort of fungus. He'd seen it growing on fish, mostly, but a tongue seemed a close enough cousin to that wet flesh. He made up his mind: *a fungus, then.*

But now a much larger question grew in his sleep-fogged brain: *How?* How could three separate species be reconciled into the shambling monstrosity he had seen? Certainly a fungus could infect a living host. He followed that thought. Hadn't he read something, in his preparation for the trip, little more than a rumor based on the field notes of a French botanist?

He chased the thought through the darkness as his hammock swayed with the ocean's motion beneath him. He was so sleepy. *Yes*, he thought, no longer struggling to get to sleep but rather to stay awake, to complete the thought.

It had been a young botanist, just out of the Sorbonne University in Paris, looking to make his name with a trip deep into the wild Amazon. There he claimed to have observed a fungus infecting ants in a most disturbing way. The fungus already growing within them, the ants had stumbled homeward, where the fungal spores had blossomed and wiped out the entire colony.

But with all that moisture and sun and shade and rot, the rain forest had plumped up the Frenchman's notebooks with dozens of exciting discoveries. The fanciful tale of a predatory fungus had earned but a few lines amid the loving descriptions of towering trees and exotic flowers, each more impressive and magnificent than the last.

In fact, it had been those tales that Henry had hoped to hear more of. "And where is this Frenchman now?" he had asked Dr. Wetherby. "Will he come to Boston, do you think, perhaps to Cambridge?"

Wetherby had looked up from his own reading on the Amazon—always a book or three ahead of his apprentice. "Not likely," he'd said. "That man is quite dead."

It had surprised Henry then, because the man had been so young. It did not surprise him now. He tried to remember those few, cryptic lines. This fungus *had* preyed on ants, but just regular ants—the kind that were a threat to picnics, perhaps, but not to people. And it had killed them quite efficiently, if he remembered correctly. He wasn't sure and couldn't reconcile any of it with what he'd seen. But then, there were so many varieties of funguses—an entire world unto themselves, really, down there among the dirt and leaves. And there was so very much that science still didn't know.

He felt sleep taking him. His eyes refused to stay open, and his limbs were weightless and numb. And what of the creature's coating—a strange and glistening substance, like a jelly or the clear white of an egg? And what of those two half-formed limbs, waving ineffectually from its midsection?

There were so many questions. Henry felt adrift and

overwhelmed as he realized he'd only been concentrating on one section of a larger puzzle. The other pieces floated just beyond his grasp, scattered and out of place. An expedition to the jungle, the boat returning half empty; a violent mutiny, and a ship abandoned; a boy's strange disappearance—and far stranger reappearance . . .

Sleep came and took him. There would be no more answers tonight. Nightmares replaced reason, and he was far from alone in that. All around him, the others indulged their own dark imaginings in the dead of night, conjuring phantoms that could hardly be more terrible than the very real transformation that was taking place between decks.

The day had barely dawned and the crew was once again churning away furiously on the chain pump. The ship had taken on a dangerous amount of water and first light found the *Polaris* riding low over the waves. With a full crew, they would have been pumping right through the storm.

The heavy old machine was operated by a pump brake, one handle rising up as the other was pushed down in a seesaw motion. With each pump another cupful of filthy bilge water would sputter up from the bottom of the hold below—and there seemed to be an endless supply. Working shoulder to shoulder, two of them could fit on each handle, four in all. There being only six of them, and one needed for the wheel, that worked well enough. The work was grueling, though, and it allowed only one of their number to rest at a time.

But almost as soon as Henry finished his first turn, collapsing onto the deck to rest, the others were already shouting at him.

"Get up," called Maria. "It's my turn to rest!"

"No, it's mine!" called Aaron.

"You are both wrong—I've been pumping the longest," insisted Thacher.

The claim made no sense. It was a four-person operation and they'd all started at the same time, except for Emma, who'd arrived late after mending something aloft.

Henry didn't waste his strength arguing, just sat against the bulwark sucking in as much air as he could. His chest rose and fell, rose and fell, in time with the pumping of the others. And then, as a fresh round of grumbling was directed his way, he rose too. He could have lingered a little longer—it wasn't as if the others could come and get him. But he wanted to do his part, and unlike sailing, this was the sort of unskilled labor to which he could actually contribute.

"All right," he wheezed. "I'm up."

He suddenly realized that he could choose who got the next break merely by sliding in to take their place. He savored his moment of power and then quickly slid into Aaron's spot.

Thacher howled in protest, allowing Maria to outmaneuver him. "I'm next!" she chirped triumphantly.

"That's not fair!" snarled Thacher.

"And I'm after her!" called Emma.

Henry's spot was next to Maria and across from Emma and Thacher. Not that it mattered. They kept their eyes down and did their best to settle into a smooth rhythm—up and down, up and down. Henry's muscles ached so badly that he wasn't sure if it was the old pump that was creaking, groaning, and sputtering, or his own body.

Even worse was the filthy brownish-gray water splashing out at their feet. Some of the cartons of food that had been stored in the hold had clearly broken down in the dampness. Little bits of spoiled food came up now and then on the round cups of the pump chain. At one point, a rat—or most of it anyway—plopped right down at Henry's feet.

Maria kicked the carcass away with her bandaged foot, but it was too late. Henry had already seen it and suddenly had to rush over to the rail to heave up over the side.

"That counts as your break!" said Thacher when he got back.

A half hour later, Owen arrived. All eyes were on him: What lucky sod would get to lean against the wheel for the rest of this? But the choice was obvious. Maria's injured foot still had not healed. *And no wonder*, thought Henry, eyeing the swampy muck she was standing in. She was putting most of her weight on her good leg, throwing off the rhythm and making the pumping more difficult for everyone.

Henry watched jealously as she headed toward the wheel, limping slightly. Then Owen started pumping, bigger and fresher than the others, and throwing off their rhythm in a whole new way.

"Settle down, you big dumb ox!" Emma called over.

Owen just smiled and pumped harder.

They went on like that until breakfast.

"Well, I don't think we'll sink," said Owen as they all washed up a bit in the ample water from the once-again-overflowing scuttlebutt. "At least not today. But we'll have to keep this pumping up, full shifts, until we reach port."

Emma had just replaced her sister at the wheel, and Henry looked down at Maria's bandaged foot. There was a splash of fresh red among the old brown stains. "You should change that wrapping," said Henry. "And wash out that wound."

Maria shrugged. "It will just get dirty again. It will heal soon enough. You'll see."

Henry wasn't so sure. *Was it so swollen the day before?* he wondered.

Aaron went to fetch the cooking pot from the little shed, passing one of the boarded-up hatches in the process. "Be careful," Henry called out after him.

The others followed Aaron's progress carefully as he passed

the hatch. There was a clang as he retrieved the pot from the shed, like the ringing of a dinner bell. Henry pictured a boy's eyes snapping open just below—a boy's eyes on a monster's body. He remembered the thorny barbs on the ends of its six twitching limbs. He looked at the thin, mismatched boards covering the hatch. What good were they against such a thing?

With mealtime upon them, they retreated to the quarterdeck, since one of them had to be back there at the wheel anyway. "There's still too much water below deck," said Owen as Aaron set up the little metal cookstove midship. "We can only get some of it with the pump. I can practically hear it sloshing around between decks. We need to get down there and bail."

"And patch the leaks," added Maria.

"And tar the hull," said Emma.

Henry stared into the distance, watching Aaron work the tinderbox to start the fire, coaxing fat sparks out of a hunk of flint and a wedge of steel.

"But we are not going to, are we?" said Maria. "Go below, I mean?"

Owen grimaced. "I suppose not," he muttered. "But we will begin the next storm already halfway to the bottom of the sea."

It had become painfully obvious that no one truly believed the creature had been killed. Nor did Henry: Where was the body? Where was the blood?

"We need to get off this ship as fast as possible," said Thacher.

This time his tone wasn't angry or argumentative. His voice was quiet and flat: He was merely stating a fact.

Owen didn't argue.

Henry considered the two boys. They weren't so different, really: both strong-willed, both capable and reasonably well educated.

The difference was that Thacher had turned to look to his left, where just over the horizon the coast of Central America was rolling slowly by. Owen had turned to look straight ahead, where over the horizon—and over the horizon after that—lay the southern coast of the United States.

The other difference was that this boat was a family business for Owen. "The silver in here belongs to my family, you know," he had said. And he could expect a handsome reward and a bright future for bringing it home. Thacher was indentured already, sold off. What did he have to lose, or to gain?

From a purely philosophical perspective, Henry found the comparison fascinating. But from a human perspective, he was fairly sure it would all end badly.

CHAPTER 20

A REVELATION FROM THE DEEP

Later that day, a fresh distraction reared its head—or their heads, rather.

"Dolphins!" called Aaron from the patched-up rail.

Henry rushed over for a look. He'd heard these creatures were uncommonly beautiful. He slowed as he neared the rail, though. The ship was pitching a bit in the waves, and there was nothing but some rope between him and a fatal ducking.

He gripped the rope tightly and peered over the side. He saw them immediately. With all its remaining sails set, the ship was kicking up a white wake as it cut through the waves, and the dolphins were cavorting at its edges as if delighted by the sight of breaking surf so far from shore.

Henry counted quickly, but just as he decided there were six of them, another one surged up from the deep to join them. He watched intently as the color of the last dolphin's skin shifted and lightened as it neared the surface and caught the sun's rays. At first it appeared green, then blue. Then it flashed all the colors of the rainbow as it broke from the water's grip and launched itself straight forward through the air. Henry gasped as the muscular marine mammal blew out a spray of mist from the blowhole atop its head.

"That one's showing off!" called Owen with delight as the dolphin splashed down.

"Look who's talking!" Emma called back, and the whole crew laughed, save for Thacher, who surveyed the action longingly from back at the wheel.

"Look at the baby!" cried Maria.

Henry swung his head back and forth until he saw it. Swimming alongside one of the dolphins, so close it could have been her shadow, was a tiny pup. It was just a few feet long, but already perfectly proportioned, an exact miniature of the rest of the pod. It swam nearly as well, tailing just a few feet behind its mother, and even rising to the surface to blow its blowhole when she did.

Henry was hypnotized by the changing colors on their backs as they surged beneath the sunlit surface. He leaned farther over the side for a closer look, clutching the makeshift rope rail tightly.

Suddenly, he felt a hard push on his shoulders.

"AAAH!" he called out as he pitched forward toward the sea.

But the same hands that had shoved his shoulders had already grabbed them tight. He swung his head around to see Aaron grinning at him.

"Why . . . you . . . simpleminded . . . shifty-eyed . . . son of a . . . cur, you . . ." Henry stammered out his insults, which only made the others laugh louder.

"Did you hear him scream?" said Maria.

"It was a shout!" protested Henry, having taken a deep breath by now. "And anyway, he could have killed me."

"Your last words would have been 'AAAH!'" said Owen, causing a fresh round of laughter.

"No," said Henry. "I would have had some words with the dolphins. I would have told them they were much better company."

They laughed again, and this time Henry joined in, satisfied that he'd acquitted himself well in the exchange. But the good mood did not last—at least not for Henry. As he turned back to the rail, the dolphins were already beginning to tire of the game. They were veering off from the boat, off to pursue fresh frolics elsewhere in the deep. Henry watched them go. The last to leave was the baby, tailing a little farther behind its mother now. *Either it has more of an appetite for play at its age*, thought Henry, *or it is just a slower swimmer.*

But a moment later, the mother dolphin slowed herself, allowing her pup to catch back up. *She's worried about it*, he thought. *So many dangers in the deep and it still so small, still only half-grown . . .*

And that's when it occurred to him. As the sunlight played

on the water before him, another much darker image flashed through his mind. He saw the creature again but not all of it. He saw its two little half-formed arms, waving ineffectually from its midsection. *Still so small, still only half-grown* . . . He remembered that strange jellylike coating dripping from their tips, and now it made sense to him. It had reminded him of the clear white of an egg, and he hadn't been far off. The whole creature was still forming, as sure as any farmyard chick. The coating was a protective salve to ease the process along.

He saw the whole creature now. The image was so clear and the realization so intense that he stumbled backward from the rail, his face slack and stricken.

"You all right there?" said Aaron. "I must've given you a greater fright than I'd planned."

Henry looked at him, blinking, trying to refocus his vision in the real world outside of his head.

"Don't you see?" he said. "The creature . . ." At the mere words, the smiles fell from the faces of the others. "It is still growing too. Growing and changing."

Henry desperately searched his mind for what he knew about ants. The first thing he thought of was their formidable strength, each one capable of carrying hundreds of times its body weight . . . *Imagine something like that the size of a person!*

Then he thought of their exoskeletons, the sheaths around their bodies, made of the same tough substance as lobster shells, an armor against the world. And how thick would that armor be on an organism of that size? *The creature's armor is still soft and wet,* he realized. It is still vulnerable, clinging to the shadows for protection as surely as that dolphin pup clings to its mother's side.

But it wouldn't be vulnerable for long.

Suddenly, he knew what they had to do.

"Don't you see?" he said, turning from one inquiring face to the next. Then, finally, he pointed to the nearest boarded-up hatch. He understood now just how pathetic a gesture it was.

"Don't you see?" he repeated.

But they didn't, and so he had to spell it out for them.

"We have to kill it *now.*"

CHAPTER 21

THE MONSTER MUST DIE

Owen listened carefully as Henry explained it all, for the second time. They had gathered around Thacher at the helm so that everyone could hear. *Lord help us all*, thought Owen, *but this frail boy is right.* He understood that Henry was smart and educated, but did he have to be so . . . He searched for the word. *Did he have to be so . . . correct?* It was maddening!

"So each day, this thing gets stronger?" said Owen.

"I believe so, yes," said Henry. "It seems to be undergoing some sort of overall transfiguration. I saw the coating—it is as the white of an egg or . . ."

"The pus upon a wound?" contributed Thacher.

"Yes," said Henry, considering it. "Unpleasant, but yes."

"But how?" asked Aaron.

"That I do not know," admitted Henry. "I am still puzzling it out. But I think it has something to do with a fungus."

"A fungus?" said Maria.

"Yes," said Henry. "Like a mushroom, that sort of thing. They reproduce by casting spores upon the wind."

"And Obed has, er, caught wind of this fungus, then?" ventured Thacher.

Henry nodded.

"But why him?" asked Emma. "Why not any of the rest of us?"

The group looked around at each other, avoiding eye contact.

"He's the one who took the doctor's chest down to the hold," said Thacher, looking up suddenly. "Your doctor's chest!" he added, pointing to Henry.

Henry was caught off guard, and Owen followed up before he could deny it. "Yes! That was the last we saw of him. Perhaps he brought this fungus back from the jungle—it certainly is not like any fungus I've ever heard of."

Henry looked pained but didn't deny it. "It is a vast and dark place, the Amazon, with countless species undiscovered."

"And remember what the old sailors whispered at night, remember the tales they told," said Thacher. "A dread disease . . ."

"And a beast in the darkness," added Maria.

"And now, it seems, we have a beast of our own," said Thacher. "But what of Obed? I saw his face—the monster was wearing it as its own. Is it still . . . *him*?"

He turned to Henry for the answer. They all did.

"Perhaps in part," he offered weakly. "How much is unknowable."

But the others refused to look away and, reluctantly, he continued. "I believe he is being consumed, taken over by this larger composite creature. He recognized the gun, for example, but he could not speak."

Owen nodded. He had seen the same thing. "So every day there will be less of him?" he said. "And more of the monster?"

"Yes," admitted Henry, "and every day the monster will be stronger: its armor thicker, its limbs longer, its claws sharper."

"But to what end?" asked Owen. "If it is no longer Obed who controls its movements, what does?"

"It must be the fungus," said Henry. "I saw it, in his mouth. It will be growing inside him as well. It is almost certainly in his brain."

"A fungus, in the brain?" said Emma, horrified. "Have you ever heard of such a thing?"

Henry nodded again. "I have. In truth, I have heard of funguses affecting the brain, causing changes in their hosts. It would not have undertaken such an elaborate transformation—such a vulnerable incubation—without a reason."

"But again, what reason?" repeated Owen. "What does it want?"

There was a heavy silence as Henry formulated his reply. Owen tried to imagine the horror of the transformation. What must it have been like for poor Obed? Did he understand what was happening to him? What was he thinking as he slowly lost control of his mind? As his body became something other—other than him, other than *human*.

"It wants the same thing as all funguses," said Henry at last. He looked up at the sails, avoiding the eyes of the others.

"And what is that?" asked Thacher.

Henry looked him directly in the eyes. He let out a long, slow breath and then spoke. "It wants to reproduce."

There was silence as the thunderstruck young crew processed this idea. The wheel slipped from Thacher's hand, and for a few stunned moments, he let it wander. By the time he'd gotten hold of it—and of himself—the ship had ventured a full two points off course.

"Oh no, no, no, no," Aaron was saying.

"But this thing's manner of reproduction," Owen mumbled, struggling to find the words for so repugnant a concept. "I mean to say, the way it goes about . . ."

"It is with other organisms," said Henry. "With people."

"And we are the only other people on this ship," whispered Emma.

Henry looked at her, then around at the others. "It will wait in the shadows. It will grow stronger. And then—"

And this time it was Owen who cut him off. "And then it will come for us."

Henry nodded. "And it will be strong, many times stronger than the strongest man. We will be powerless to halt its advance. Wood, rope, even steel: Nothing we have would stop it."

"But what of the gun?" said Owen, looking down toward the pistol at his belt.

"I don't know," said Henry. "Think of an ant . . ."

"A bullet would smash it!" declared Aaron triumphantly.

"Now think of an ant the size of a man, its external skeleton perhaps several inches thick and harder than the horns of a bull."

"Oh," said Aaron, slumping visibly.

"So we must strike now," said Owen.

Henry looked up at him. Owen had hoped to see resolve in his eyes—grim determination for what needed to be done and certainty as to how to go about it. Instead, he saw only resignation and sadness.

"If it is not already too late," said Henry. "But we must try at least. Either it lives or we do. The ship is too small. It cannot be both."

There was silence, save for the whipping wind.

It was Owen who broke the spell this time. "Then it will be us," he said firmly.

His bluster energized the others.

"The monster must die!" cheered Thacher.

"Huzzah!" called Emma.

Maria set the plans in motion. "We must fetch weapons," she said. "Anything to strike at it."

Owen saw her turn and take a few steps, off to fetch some sharpened thing or other. But he also saw her wince as she put her weight on her swollen and bandaged foot, and he saw her limp as she dragged it forward for another painful step.

"Not you, Maria," he said.

She turned back toward him, pivoting on her good foot. "What do you mean?" she protested. "I must do my part. I was a bullfighter in a past life!"

Owen had no idea how to respond to that. *A bullfighter?* "You would only slow us down," he said after a few seconds of silence. "And I believe you might be of more service up here."

"At the wheel, you mean?"

He looked up at the sails and then out at the horizon. The wind was light but steady and the seas mild. The wheel wasn't fighting Thacher, particularly. Owen shook his head. "No, we can risk tying the wheel off again, at least for a bit," he said. "We can fashion other instruments for you, deadlier ones . . ."

Maria smiled. He guessed that the bullfighter in her liked that idea.

He smiled back, but it was forced. The wind was in the sails. The way was clear. They had food and water. It was going well, if you could ignore the fact that the boat was taking on water—sinking as it went—and there was an armor-plated, fungus-brained monster growing stronger each day and waiting to turn them all into its kin. He sighed heavily as Maria took the wheel.

And so they began to make their preparations to go below once more. Eyeing the sun above, working quickly but with great care. It wouldn't be their first trip between decks. But this time, he knew, they wouldn't be avoiding this fierce creature.

They would be hunting it.

CHAPTER 22

THE HUNT

The sun had passed its peak and begun its slow slide toward evening.

The five healthy members of the ship's crew were about to head down too.

Owen stood at the mouth of the freshly opened aft hatch. Bent nails and discarded boards were neatly stacked nearby. The lantern in his left hand glowed uselessly in the sunlight, as the pistol in his right pointed down into the dark expanse below. He risked a quick look forward. "Keep your eyes open and your ears apeak," he called to Maria, where she knelt among her weaponry. "Our very lives are at stake!"

She looked up at him, put her hands on either side of her head, and extended her index fingers upward.

"She is imitating a bull," explained Emma, who was standing just behind Owen.

"I thought she was a bullfighter," he said, confused.

"To the Spanish, it is all one."

Owen shook his head, baffled.

"Are you two going to stand there out in the open all day?"

called Thacher, third in line. After listening to Henry's explanation of the monster's exoskeleton, he had replaced the gaff hook he'd carried during their last venture between decks with a hatchet.

"We are not trying to sneak up on the thing," Owen reminded Thacher. "We want it to come for us."

He said it bravely enough, but his thoughts were far less bold. "Lord help us all," he whispered as he turned and headed down the ladder. *First in line,* he thought. *First to die?*

But there were no onrushing claws to greet him as he reached the bottom, only ankle-deep water that he found nearly as alarming.

He stepped aside and made way for Emma, then Thacher, Henry, and Aaron.

For a while, they all stood there in the sloshing water and squared-off sunlight.

"It would be better, all things considered, if the creature came to us," said Owen.

"That is true," said Henry. "But it is impossible, as yet, to ascertain its manner of predation."

Owen had no idea what that meant, but as they were in no hurry, he asked this learned boy one last question that had been on his mind. "Why an ant? I mean to say, if this thing is a fungus, and this fungus has attacked Obed Macy, then why is it a monstrous insect we are hunting and not, for example, a boyish mushroom?"

"That is a fine question," said Henry, raising his voice as he answered. *Whatever his answer is,* thought Owen, *I am glad he understands the dangerous waiting game we are playing. To be heard, to be seen . . .*

"It is a parasite, and I believe the ant is the species it usually targets," began Henry. "There must be some strong connection between the two. After preying on ants for so long, the fungus seems to have—how do I put this?—taken on their essential characteristics, perhaps?"

"Their essential what?" said Aaron, who had affixed a long iron spike to the end of a mop handle and was now waving the improvised spear toward the darkness.

Henry, who was carrying a thick-handled torch as both a weapon and a source of light, went on. "There is a theory, gaining some ground of late, concerning the transmutation of species over time. Changes with each successive generation—that sort of thing. I do wish the doctor were still with us to explain it better. I do not know enough—and am too scared, at present, to think intelligently."

Owen snorted and then regretted it instantly. At the very least, he admired the boy's honesty. And if the botanist's assistant had been rendered stupid, where did that leave the cabin boy? Still, Owen thought he just might understand something that his scientific crew mate did not.

The realization came to him from an unlikely place: a

summer day years before, spent at the beach with his mother. He'd been seven then, or perhaps eight. He could no longer remember his exact age with certainty, but the rest of the details were stamped indelibly into his mind. It was the sort of strong childhood memory that people carry to their graves.

His mother had been wearing a puffy, striped bathing gown that covered her from ankle to neck. He'd been wearing his own two-piece bathing outfit, complete with a navy-blue top and a simple belt to keep his shorts up in the waves. They were kicking about in the warm shallows of low tide when his mother had called out, "Look, look! It is about to happen!"

Owen had rushed over to the stone lip of a little tidal pool and looked where she pointed. What he saw there was a hermit crab, about the size of his thumbnail. He'd seen them many times before, of course, but never before had he seen one naked! The alien-looking little beast had just pulled itself free of its old shell. Owen watched in astonishment as it scampered across the wet stone and into a larger shell it had pulled up nearby. The little crab quickly turned itself around inside its new shell and popped its head and legs back out the front. Without a moment's hesitation, it walked right off the lip of the tidal pool and plopped down into the shallow sea.

Owen had stared at the abandoned shell. Once the hard back of a crab, it was now just another shell. "It outgrew it, you see," his mother said. "It could barely fit inside—or pry itself loose—and so it needed to find a larger shell. It needed a new home, just as we shall, when your little brother or sister arrives."

His mother had straightened up as Owen looked at her belly, bulging out beneath her gown. He'd nodded then, thinking he understood. And he had understood—about the crab, at least. What he didn't know was that his younger brother, for he would have been a brother, would never arrive. Not really. He would die in the process of being born.

Just as his mother would die in the process of giving birth.

Owen was glad he hadn't known that then.

He was certain that the same sort of thing was happening here. The creature they were hunting was a parasite. He knew what that meant. He'd had some schooling too, even if most of it was on board this ship. A parasite was an opportunist, a scrounger: a tick growing fat on a dog's hide.

And this one was a fungus. With no feet of its own, it would rely on some other creature to carry it. And after all those years in the jungle, relying on ants to carry it short distances, it had simply found a better home. It had sought out a bigger home— just as the crab had—one with longer legs to carry it farther.

As his eyes probed the dim belly of the ship, he saw a bit of light from the open grating midway down the passageway. That was the one they were aiming for. He raised the lantern and held it out in front of him as one final thought made his blood run cold. This creature had found not only longer legs to carry it, but tall sails as well. If this horrid species spread, he realized, the *Polaris* would be the vessel that spread it.

They had to kill the monster before they reached land—and before it killed them.

Owen set his jaw and steadied his hand. "Come out, you fiend!" he called into the dull, wet hollow before him. "Come out and get what's coming to you!"

There was no response. The only sound was the water sloshing at their feet and the gentle waves slapping against the hull.

"It must know we're here by now," said Henry.

"Aye, it knows," said Owen.

Is it possible that the monster understands it must leave this ship to survive? he wondered. *Is the creature blotting out the brain of its human host, or taking it over?*

Whatever the case, it was clearly too smart to come charging straight into the wall of weaponry currently deployed against it.

"We're going to have to go look for it, aren't we?" said Aaron.

Owen sized up the dim passageway before them. Amid the shadows and flickering firelight, an opening in the bulkhead wall formed a dark square. It was hot, stuffy, and almost unbearably humid between decks, but the opening chilled him like a plunge into icy water. It was a natural bottleneck, an obvious ambush point, and they would have to go through it. He knew the longer they waited, the harder it would be.

"No time like the present," he said, taking a deep breath.

"Remember, if we encounter it amidships, we are to draw it to the grating there."

"Or it might meet us there, like last time," offered Emma.

"One can hope," said Owen, though he knew it was a strange thing to hope for.

Slowly, they began moving forward; a few of them were looking back as they did so. Their weapons were pointed out in all directions, like the quills of a porcupine. Owen felt the sweat pouring from him in the swampy heat.

"Maybe it really is dead," ventured Aaron.

Owen only grunted. He had advanced the idea himself, and he really ought to put an end to it now. But that was another bone-deep memory, another one to take to the grave. He remembered his hand shaking with fear as he pulled the trigger and then jerking upward with the blast—it had been so long since he'd fired a pistol! The recoil had been far greater than he recalled. It was true that, when the smoke cleared, the monster was gone. But if they wanted to find the bullet, he felt fairly certain they'd be better off searching the wooden ceiling than the monster's belly.

"Keep your eyes open," he growled, as close as he could come to an admission.

"Not about to close 'em now," grumbled Aaron.

Owen didn't answer. They had reached the dark gap in the bulkhead. "Ready yourselves," he said, and then he pushed through with a little hop. Water splashed at his feet and his pulse pounded as he swung the lantern and pistol from side to side. But the passage was narrow here, and the flickering lantern light revealed nothing but dark walls and shut doors.

"All clear," he said in one long exhale.

As they continued on, the passage opened back up. Once again it stretched the width of the ship. They reached the open grating midship and called up to let Maria know they'd arrived. Weak light filtered in as they passed beneath. A strange mix of light and shadows bewitched Owen's vision, torchlight behind, lantern light in front, and daylight all around. The shadows danced back and forth, and the light glittered on the water at his feet. Everything seemed to be moving, even the walls.

Owen felt his pulse race again, the drumbeat in his ears drowning out the sound of his companions.

The crew berth was just up ahead, swamped now with sloshing water. Owen realized he'd been holding his breath, anticipating the funk of all that discarded wool and grimy leather awash in filthy brine. Reluctantly, he sucked in a quick breath. But it wasn't old boots and wet trousers he smelled. Once again, it was something much sweeter.

"Oh no," he gasped.

"It's here," whispered Thacher just behind him.

Panic flooded Owen's brain and suddenly he couldn't for the life of him remember why they had *wanted* to be attacked. He did not want that *at all* now!

"Where?" whispered Emma.

Owen swung his lantern from side to side in front of them. As the light chased away the shadows, he saw nothing out of the ordinary. Perhaps in the darkness just beyond? He took another breath and his lungs filled with the sweet stench of what he now knew to be a predatory fungus. He wanted to retch.

Then, a sound.

Owen heard a soft scratching directly above him. His first thought was that they had left the hatch open and perhaps the monster had escaped to the deck. But as he looked up, he understood that it hadn't gone anywhere.

It was directly above them.

The light of both torch and lantern played across its dark red back. Its six barbed legs were spread wide and secured firmly into the wood. And then its head swung around.

All the way around.

It considered them through the eyes of Obed Macy.

Gone was the layer of gelatinous slime that had coated his face before. All that was left was a dewy gloss, like a light sweat.

Several of the crew shouted and screamed at once.

"What is happening?" Maria called down through the grating behind them, but no one answered her.

The group scattered outward in a rough circle, and the creature released its grip and dropped down into their midst. As Owen watched, the thing flipped over in midair. It landed on all six legs with a soft splash and a loud thud. The middle legs, he saw, were now as long as the others. *It has grown*, he realized. *It has matured.*

Trembling, Owen struggled to draw back the hammer of his pistol.

The monster rose from its belly and stood on its two hind legs. Its antennas nearly touched the ceiling.

Click. The hammer of the pistol locked into place.

Once again, Obed's face swung around. His eyes locked onto Owen's.

"Fire, Owen!" called Thacher, just off to his left, his hatchet raised.

The creature was outlined against the light of Henry's torch. It had grown tall but thin, with bulbous sections at its chest and hips connected by a thin, almost-dainty waist. And clearly visible behind it were Henry and Aaron, cut off from the others and seemingly paralyzed with fright.

"I can't risk it!" yelled Owen. He had only one shot and no longer entertained any delusions of accuracy. "Give ground, you two!"

Aaron stood like a statue, his improvised spear held directly out in front of him. Henry's eyes were as round as silver dollars, and he was waving his torch vaguely in the monster's direction.

Curse them, thought Owen. *Who would have thought those two would need to be told twice to flee?*

He raised his trembling gun hand and aimed for the round red ball of the thing's chest. He reminded himself of the recoil this time. "Exhale and fire," he whispered, repeating the advice he'd received when he'd first learned to shoot.

But before Owen had even finished the phrase, the creature kicked one of its powerful standing legs forward. A bucket's worth of filthy salt water splashed across Owen's face and his chest and, worst of all, his gun.

He pulled the trigger. The hammer fell forward and landed with a solid metallic clack! But there was no spark, no fire. *Is the pan wet? Is the powder?*

Owen looked quickly down at the pistol and then back up at the creature. It cocked its head to the side and *smiled*. It was a terrible smile, not because it was monstrous, but because it was still so human.

It didn't help that Obed's teeth had turned quite black now.

Owen swallowed hard. He would have to try again, but before he could even get his thumb on the hammer, the creature rushed forward.

On either side of Owen, Thacher and Emma fell back toward their respective walls. Thacher hacked at the air with his hatchet, and Emma lashed out wildly with a knife in each hand now.

One of them made contact. Owen heard a quick sound behind him—*tik-taclik!*—like metal on bone.

Which one, he couldn't say, as he was now running head-long back toward the open grating.

The monster ignored the others and whatever minor wound it had sustained and rushed after him, dropping down to four legs to increase its speed. It was pursuing the greatest threat.

"Now, Maria!" Owen shouted as he passed under the grating.

"Watch out!" she called back down.

A moment later, boiling water poured down through the square openings. The wood hissed and steamed were the water hit it. Maria had done her job well and kept the cooking pot at a rolling boil, and now the scalding water slapped down on the back of the charging creature.

It released a muffled cry and lurched to the side, colliding against a thick wooden column with a dull crack.

"I think I got it!" crowed Maria.

Stunned by the collision, the creature rose unsteadily to all six feet. Then it turned its head around to look at its wound. In the streaming sunlight, Owen saw steam rising from the thing's back. A section just above its waist had turned a bright, cooked-lobster red.

Obed's face was a twisted mix of pain and anger. As soon as his eyes found the steaming burn wound, the creature flopped over onto its back. There was one last quick hiss as its back landed in the sloshing wastewater.

Owen used the opportunity to edge back around the squirming insectoid and rejoin his mates. He called up to Maria once again. "Get the spear!"

Shimmying on its back like a cat rolling on a rug, the creature opened its eyes wide. It twisted quickly to one side, legs scrambling for purchase. Just as it righted itself, there was a flash of metal directly above it.

It leapt toward the darkness beyond the grating.

The point of the spear shot straight down. It missed the creature's bulbous hindquarters by inches and sunk into the wood with a dull thunk.

The creature landed in the shadows a moment later. From the edge of the light, it peered up toward the grating. Maria's shape was visible through the openings as she wrestled with the spear, trying to free it from the floor.

"Be careful, Maria!" Emma called up. "It's watching you."

The spear came loose with one final tug and Maria began hauling it up. "Where is it?" she called. "I won't miss this time!"

Meanwhile, Owen and the others had regrouped on the other side of the light. Once again, they faced forward, a solid wall of weaponry. "It is injured," whispered Owen. "We must charge it."

Click. The hammer of his pistol locked into place.

Without even looking down, the creature leaned back out of the light, and suddenly it was gone.

"I can't see it anymore," said Aaron.

Suddenly, there was a slap of wood and a rush of draining water.

"NOOOO!" bellowed Owen, rushing forward. His lantern was held out at arm's length and his pistol was held in close to his body. He rushed through the light from the grating.

The others followed, not as a unified wall anymore, but more like a line of ducklings, each one more reluctant than the one before. "Don't spear me!" Emma called as she passed under her sister's shadow.

Owen reached the edge of the light and plunged forward into the darkness. It was a huge risk, but if they didn't stop the monster now, he doubted they ever would.

Thunk!

Owen reached his destination and came to a halt. He held the lantern out and stared at the raised hatch and the heavy wooden door at its center.

Emma arrived, then Thacher, and then Henry and Aaron.

"Did it?" asked Emma.

Owen nodded. "It escaped down into the hold."

"Should we, uh, go after it?" asked Henry.

"It would be suicide," said Thacher. "It is a lightless hole, cramped and crammed with every manner of obstacle and impediment. And now it will be flooded, the cargo toppled over, everything in disarray. It would be dangerous, honestly, even without a monster."

The assembled crew stood looking at the wooden hatch. No one questioned Thacher's assessment. The hold had been his domain once. Now it belonged to the beast.

Images played out in Owen's head. They had drawn the creature out into the open. They had sprung their trap. Their plan had worked.

And yet the monster still lived.

Now it would complete its transformation in darkness.

CHAPTER 23

DARK DAYS

As the crew mulled over its failure for the next few days, the weather seemed to be trying to lift their spirits. The skies were blue, and there was a steady wind out of the southeast. But no amount of tropical sunshine could brighten their moods now. Their thoughts had turned stormy, and their prospects for survival had turned dark.

They did what they could to improve their situation. They boarded up the hatches again. They fortified the door to the cabin, in case they needed one last refuge to retreat to.

"It won't matter, you know," Henry had said as he held out another nail for Owen to hammer in. "Once the creature is at full strength—with six barbed legs, each as strong as a kicking mule—it will tear through this wood like a sparrow flying through a spiderweb. It is only a matter of time—and not much of it either."

Owen mumbled, "It might matter," and then promptly smashed his thumb with the hammer.

As the sun rose and fell and the shadows stretched and retreated, the crew jumped at every sudden sound. On a ship whose wood and steel constantly groaned and thumped, their nerves stretched thinner and thinner. And the hardships didn't end there. They cut their rations in half, by more or less general agreement. The food they had would have to last now—unless maybe they could pull some from the sea. And at the first hint of rain, every bucket and pan they had was set up to catch the fresh water.

Now they were hungry as well as sore. The enormous task of sailing the ship alone was made harder still by grumbling stomachs and a lack of energy. The little cleaning and maintenance they'd kept up with was abandoned. If they ever did get the *Polaris* into port, she wouldn't be a pretty sight.

Neither would her crew. A quick rain shower swept across the sea on the third day after the failed hunt. The crew scrambled to collect the water, but not one of them made a move to grab a bit of soap for a long-overdue cleaning. Their hair grew matted and clumped. Their faces were streaked and greasy. And their clothes, which had been grimy for some time already, descended into indecency.

"What is that smell?" asked Aaron during a brief lull in the wind.

Thacher looked up from where he sat, sharpening his hatchet. "It is us," he said, waving the blade around in a menacing circle. "It is all of us."

The wind had picked up again after that, mercifully

scattering the odor. But the wind gained strength and its mercy was short-lived. Soon the ragged crew had to scramble up into the rigging to take in more sail before something else on the neglected ship broke or tore.

Once again, Henry had barely reached the top by the time the others were descending to the next sail. Owen balanced against the forward topsail yard, grabbing canvas by the fistful and considering the frail boy. It wasn't a lack of experience at this point; it was a lack of aptitude. Henry simply would never be an accomplished sailor. What bothered Owen most about it was knowing that, apart from some wounded pride, Henry didn't care one bit. Owen saw the way the other boy's eyes searched the horizon for land. He wanted nothing more than to be back on solid ground, likely for the rest of his life.

Owen longed to reach port too, of course. That was the only path to survival. But the sea, and this ship, was his home. His uncle had taken him in after his mother's death and his father's descent into sorrow—and the bottle. The *Polaris* had given him a place and a purpose.

He would return to shore but not to stay. He looked forward to reaching safe harbor for a time: There would be men and guns there—the army, perhaps. Whatever it took to wipe their foul cargo from the face of the earth. And afterward, there would be a heap of strong lye soap to scrub its memory from the sturdy old wood of the *Polaris*.

Who would take over the ship then? Who could say? But Owen felt sure his family would have some say in the matter. And whoever it was, surely they would need a steady cabin boy who knew the boat inside and out.

So, yes, he would bring the *Polaris* into port, but it had to be a safe one. It had to be in the United States, where the laws of property and inheritance would be respected and upheld.

Unfortunately, even with kind winds, the U.S. was still far beyond the horizon. They were still sailing across the blue waters of the Caribbean Sea, and not everyone shared his conviction to see the journey through. The talk had started up again as soon as they had returned from their ill-fated trip between decks.

"We must steer for the nearest port," said Thacher. "Those who meet us may not be of our nationality, but at least they will be of our *species*."

And he was far from alone in that position. In fact, as the days wore on, it was Owen who was beginning to feel more and more isolated.

The idea of organized watches fell by the wayside. The pumping took up more and more time, and still the ship rode lower and lower in the water. There was simply too much work to do and too few of them to do it.

No one worked harder than Owen, but having been on deck for much of the night and all of the day, he pulled the captain's spare pocket watch from his trousers and noted the passing of another four hours. His watch was at least technically over. With the sails in good shape and no need to adjust sheet or stay, he finally slunk back into the cabin for a few hours of sleep. He took one last look over at the helm. *Can I trust the others to stay the course?* He yawned. He would have to.

The light was dim as he entered and the air was thick with the smell of his crew mates, even though none of them were currently there. He wanted nothing more than to stumble over to his hammock and let the sea rock him to sleep, but he forced himself over to the desk first. He wanted to double-check their heading one more time. They could not afford to waste time correcting their route later.

He turned up the lantern above the desk and took a seat. As soon as he was off his feet, his body seemed to collapse. His eyes drifted closed; his head drooped down . . .

Owen snapped back awake. He forced his eyes to open wide and shook his sleep-fogged head. *Check the course first*, he told himself. *Then sleep.*

He had to dig hard into his memory for the observations he'd taken on deck just a minute earlier. He reached for the map blindly as he looked over toward the big compass, floating level in its gimbal as the ship gently rose and fell.

His hand searched the desk for the map, but he didn't feel it there. Strange. He let his hand hop around to either side.

"Ow!" he yelped, feeling a sharp jab in his palm. He turned his eyes from the compass and toward the desk. He had stabbed himself on a V-shaped device known as a divider.

"What is that doing there?" he mumbled to himself.

And then he saw the map, pushed halfway up the desktop and folded over in entirely the wrong way.

He sprang to his feet and raced toward the door, the fog of sleep burning off under the sudden searing heat of anger. *Someone has been fooling with the navigation equipment!* Owen fumed at the thought: He had forbidden it! They had all agreed!

Marks had been made on that map, pins and clips affixed at exactly the right spots—and not just by him but also by the captain himself! And those dividers had been opened to exactly the right width to check the next measurement against the last.

Three words burned in his brain as he barreled through the door: *Who did this?*

The door slammed hard against the wall and Owen took in the entire scene at a glance. Thacher was leaning in close to Aaron, just past the quarterdeck. At the sound of the door, they both wheeled around and looked straight at him. Their eyes were wide, but he didn't think it was fear he saw there. It was something else. And when they both looked down, avoiding his angry gaze, he knew what.

Guilt.

They'd been caught talking behind his back. It was a common enough occurrence aboard a sailing ship, where gossip and slander abounded and no one was ever too far from anyone else.

He was sure they were talking about him. He headed straight toward them. Thacher's eyes rose sheepishly, but they didn't meet his. Instead, they lingered on the gun stuck in his belt.

"What is it?" said Maria from over at the wheel.

Her voice was innocent enough, without being too innocent, and he made up his mind then that she was not a part of it. He reached the edge of the little quarterdeck but did not descend the steps. Instead, he stood there, glaring down at the other two.

"Who's been at the maps?" he snarled. "They're a mess—a wreck! I think we've lost some of the markings!"

He stared daggers at them as he said it, trying to make them understand the seriousness of the situation. Navigation was a complex business, relying not just on compass readings and star sightings but also math and intuition. Owen had poured every bit of his brain into it and had nearly gone cross-eyed staring at the maps and charts. He had swum upstream against the wizardry of Bowditch's *Practical Navigator*. And if he felt he had made some headway, if he had gained some small confidence that they were on the right course, it was just barely. And now to have his work upended? And for what?

"Where are the others?" he demanded, but a moment later

he saw Emma aloft—of course—and Henry bungling Lord knows what task on the forecastle.

He turned his attention back to Thacher and Aaron, sure it was one of them. He spat out his next words like poisoned pellets: "Who. Did. This?"

Thacher finally looked up. He made glancing eye contact with Owen and broke into a small, maddening smile. "Perhaps it was Daffy?" he said.

"The ship's cat?" sputtered Owen.

"Why not?" said Thacher. "She can't go below to catch rats anymore. Maybe she got restless and made a mess of the desk?"

Owen glared at him. "Aye, maybe she did jump up there," he said. "But tell me: When did she learn to use a divider?"

Thacher looked down. "She is an exceedingly clever cat," he said to his own sun-browned bare feet.

Owen heard a soft chuckle from Aaron and felt his face growing hot and his pulse pounding in his ears.

"But tell me," Thacher continued, "not having seen the maps, I don't know for sure, but are we not nearing some large ports?"

Owen felt like his head was going to explode. "So that's what this is about," he muttered bitterly. Thacher had pored over the maps trying to find the nearest ports. The betrayal felt like a punch in the gut. Owen desperately wanted to leap down and throttle Thacher into unconsciousness—and then wake him up by tossing him overboard.

"Perhaps just a bit north of here?" added Aaron.

Owen glared at him, his eyes narrowed into slits. "You too, Aaron?"

"Me too, what?" said Aaron, his voice dripping with fake innocence.

Owen shook his head and looked up to the sky. It was useless. He saw the pale gray sails stretched tight with wind and Emma moving high up through the rigging like a spider. He could prove nothing—and who would he prove it to? There was no greater authority left. No captain to order them chained up below, no first mate to whip their backs raw.

There was just him—and he was so tired now. He felt his pounding pulse soften and the blood draining from his head. His shoulders slumped.

And what punishment could he possibly threaten that was greater than what they already faced? By hand or claw or sea, they would all be punished.

Punished for the deeds of others, punished for forces beyond their control. It didn't seem fair. He looked at Thacher once more, sizing him up. He noticed that he was now wearing a hatchet in the same place that Owen himself wore his gun.

Punished for the deeds of others, he thought again. *But maybe we will have committed some crimes of our own by then.*

CHAPTER 24

UNEASY AT THE WHEEL

That night, Owen was standing at the wheel. The moon was nearly full and the sky was cloudless. The deck glowed silver all around him. He looked up at the sails, shimmering in all that moonlight. *They'd be prettier with more wind in them*, he thought. The wind had dropped off now, and the heavy ship was making slow progress through the night.

Once again, he tried to calculate how much longer the voyage would take. They were nearing Cuba now, if he had it figured correctly. He knew three things about the island: It was ruled by Spain, produced a tremendous amount of sugar cane, and was quite close to the tip of Florida. That was their target. If they'd had the time and crew, they would bring the ship back to the teeming ports of New York or Boston. But they had neither, so Florida would have to do.

He ran through what he knew of that place too. It was a U.S. territory now. Some said it would become a state soon, but others said that day was still a long way off. There had been trouble in Florida recently, fighting between the army and the native population. But there were ports there, with deep harbors. The closest was at Key West. If they could skirt the western edge of Cuba, they could turn east and head straight there.

His hands light on the wheel, his eyes drifted over to the aft hatch, still boarded up tight as a drum. They just needed a little more time. He looked up at the drooping sails. *A little more time, and a little more wind . . .*

A thought occurred to him. They could go back on full rations tomorrow. They were close enough, and he was reasonably sure there was enough food left. With the ship going so slowly, they had even managed to catch a few fat fish. Maybe more food would ease the tensions and quiet some of the conspiratorial whispering.

The only person he was sure was on his side was Henry. If Owen understood correctly, he wanted to bring the ship back to the United States out of some loyalty to his former employer. Owen wasn't sure exactly why, but he was glad for the support. Though he was an abysmal sailor, Henry enjoyed a certain status among the crew as the leading authority on the creature lurking below.

But Thacher agitated constantly for heading to port and had moaned and groused at every one that passed by unseen, from Kingston on one side to Belize Town on the other. Aaron was quieter about it but had made his allegiance clear enough. Maria had too, though he could hardly blame her for that. She was in constant pain now because of her infected foot and welcomed the thought of a doctor of any nationality.

Emma had yet to declare her loyalty. He hoped that she backed him and was simply staying silent to avoid an argument with her sister. He thought Emma trusted him, maybe even admired him a little . . . He pictured her now, climbing nimbly up the shrouds.

Owen tugged hard on the wheel, as if it were the ship that had wandered off course and not his thoughts.

Focus, he told himself. *It is the others I need to convince.* Even if Emma was on his side, it would still be three for and three against. If she wasn't, the numbers would be against him. Regardless, he knew there would be tremendous pressure to make landfall in Cuba once they sighted it. He'd have to make sure he was at the wheel then. Or Henry—but then they might crash into shore anyway.

And maybe it was the thought of land so close, passing just off the starboard bow. Or maybe it was the realization that most of the others disagreed with the course he'd set. Whatever the case, a troubling new thought sprang to mind. It was simple enough but utterly explosive to him. Four words that he had very rarely entertained before: *What if I'm wrong?*

The thought was new to him, but the image they brought to mind was quite familiar. He whispered a name into the night air. It was the name of an old sailor. It was the name, he now realized, of the first victim of the strange contagion that the *Polaris* now carried in its hold.

"Wrickitts."

He remembered the changes that had come over him: the shambling gait, like the creature's, the "perfume" smell, the grotesque rash. He shuddered to think where those changes would have led had they been left to run their course. He remembered the mutineers' words through the door: "Look at him!" And then a gunshot and the shouted order to pitch his ravaged body overboard.

They'd wanted to rid the ship of him—and to rid the world of the ship. They were the villains who had killed his beloved captain.

But what if they were right?

CHAPTER 25

DAFFY RAISES THE ALARM

Henry lay awake for most of the night. He was sure he heard something moving just below the cabin. The wind had picked up again, and he strained to isolate the sound from the gentle hush-hush of the ship rolling through the water and the not-so-gentle snoring of Aaron in the next hammock. *There!* He heard it again. Was it a scratch? A thump? *It's both*, he decided, and went back to listening. His heart hammered in his chest. It was coming from directly below them. Was it a coincidence, or could the creature sense their presence through the worn old wood?

You don't even know if it is the creature, he told himself. Calm down. Be reasonable.

But it didn't work. He was sure it was the creature—he could practically see its barbed feet dragging across the wet wood below. *How deep is the water between decks now? And when will the creature tire of its dreary confinement there?*

He went back to listening but only heard the noise once more that night. And he was so sleepy that he wondered if he'd dreamed it. Because the noise had changed. It almost sounded like the scratching was coming from within the floor, not below it.

Finally he drifted off to sleep. Almost immediately he was woken up to take his turn at the pumps. He groaned and headed out along with Aaron. The chain pump worked better with four people but the job could be done with two. Henry's muscles still ached from the day before. His muscles always seemed to ache these days. *Look on the bright side*, he told himself. *At least you have muscles now.*

The moon was low and sunrise near as he and Aaron padded wordlessly across the gently rolling deck. Henry had no trouble keeping his balance in conditions like this now and had even adopted the same loose-hipped, rolling gait that served the others so well. The one thing he still could not do well was climb the rigging to work the sails. The reason for that had less to do with the sea than the sky, though. He had discovered, much to his embarrassment, that he was terrified of heights.

He took up his position on the pump. "Ready?" he asked, grasping the handle.

"No," grumbled Aaron, following it with a big, open-mouthed yawn.

"Too bad," said Henry. "I think this boat is near to sinking." He raised up, preparing to push his side of the handle down.

But Aaron didn't lift his handle. Instead, he fixed his gaze on Henry, who peered back at him in the dim dawn light. "This old boat *is* near to sinking, and we need to get it off the waves," he said, his sleepiness replaced with an icy seriousness. "One more storm'll be the end of us."

Henry held his gaze. "We will get her off the waves soon enough. We can't be too far from Florida now."

"There's other land that's closer," said Aaron. "And it's not just the waves. Every minute we're on board with that thing is a minute too long. You said it yourself: These barriers"—he lifted his chin toward the boarded-up forward hatch—"cannot hold it back."

"But we haven't heard from it in days," Henry began, but he stopped there, unwilling to lie further to his only real friend on board. He had, after all, heard from the thing just hours before.

"But every day we don't hear from it, it grows stronger," said Aaron. "You said that too."

Henry nodded. He had said that, but his thoughts on the matter had shifted dramatically of late—and not in ways he felt comfortable sharing. He searched his sleepy brain for something he could say. "We gave it a good scalding last time, though. It may fear us. Bugs are, after all, quite dumb."

Aaron snorted. "That thing's no bug."

Henry remembered the look in the Obed Macy's eyes when Owen first pointed the pistol. *True again*, he thought. All he could think to do now was change the subject. "Well," he said, "if we don't start pumping soon, we won't have to worry about it."

Aaron smirked. "You're such a schoolmarm sometimes," he said, bending down to grasp the pump handle.

"Ready?" said Henry.

Aaron nodded, and the two got to work. They pumped steadily as the moon set, took a brief break to watch the sun rise, and then got back to it as the sky lightened above them. It would have been beautiful, if not for the rancid bilge water splashing at their feet.

Henry's top half was soaked with sweat and his bottom half wet with bilge by the time Thacher and Maria showed up to relieve them. Henry was desperate for a drink of water and watched their approach eagerly. They seemed to take forever to cross the deck. Maria was limping badly now, and Thacher was all too happy to slow his pace to match hers.

"You should change that bandage again when you are done here," Henry said as Maria hobbled her way to his side of the pump.

She shrugged. "I'm not sure I want to see what is underneath," she said.

"What she needs is a doctor, not fresh rags," said Thacher.

Aaron and Maria nodded emphatically at that.

"Perhaps you could talk some sense into our little dictator," Thacher continued. "He seems to respect your opinion." He thought about that and then clarified, "Not about sailing, of course, but about matters scientific."

Henry looked around. He was outnumbered, and it made him uncomfortable. "Perhaps," he said lamely, and headed straight for the scuttlebutt to plug his lying mouth with a cup of cool water. Because he knew he would say nothing of the sort to Owen. He agreed with Owen. They did need to reach the United States. The creature they were carrying with them might be a horrible thing, but Henry realized something else now.

It was also a truly amazing discovery.

The others had felt despair when they failed to kill it. Henry had felt relief. The creature terrified him, but the thought of its destruction now scared him nearly as much.

It was an entirely new form of life: a hybrid organism, a fungus capable of a metamorphosis far more intricate than any butterfly's. It was the intersection of three different fields of biology. Who knew what scientific advances it might lead to? Henry's mind raced at the possibilities.

And Dr. Wetherby had discovered this terrible, marvelous thing. It was his last and greatest contribution to science. It was his legacy. Henry was confident that a properly trained customs official could be made to understand that. The U.S. government had, after all, provided some of the funds for this research expedition. The creature must not be burned as a monster, but rather studied as a marvel. Perhaps they would even name this new species after Wetherby. *What a way to honor his memory.* The cooling water spilled down his chin as his face bent into a crooked smile.

He cast his eyes around the deck. Owen was talking quietly to Emma near the helm. They both had on their broad black hats to shield against the morning sun.

Suddenly, Henry caught a quick movement out of the corner of his left eye and heard a soft rustling. He whipped his head around toward the heavy storm tarpaulin that had been stretched over the nearest grating. He was almost sure he'd seen a flicker of movement there. He stared at it as he wiped his hand across his mouth and chin.

"What are you looking at?" said Aaron, lifting up the water cup for his turn.

Henry flinched but managed to collect himself. "Nothing," he said. "Thought I saw the cover move. The wind, most likely."

"Aye," said Aaron. "Guess we're all a little jumpy now."

"Guess so," said Henry, but his words were punctuated by the soft rustle of the tarp.

He turned once again, and this time he did see something. Daffodil was advancing slowly toward a coil of old rope that had been left on the far side of the grating cover. "Oh, it's just Daffy," Henry said to Aaron.

Henry watched her move. She was crouched down low in front, with her head just over her paws. Her tail flicked silently back and forth. *Is she hunting something?*

"Get that, will you?" said Aaron.

"The cat?"

"No, the rope. We need it to mend the rigging—and someone'll trip over it if we leave it there, anyhow."

"Oh, right," said Henry, hopping over the corner of the

grating cover and eyeing the coil of rope. Someone could definitely turn an ankle if they stepped in the dark hollow at its center.

He brushed past Daffy and bent down to give her a scratch behind the ears. She avoided him, bending around his hand and continuing to stalk slowly toward the coil.

"Hunting rope, are you?" said Henry.

He straightened up and continued on toward their mutual objective. Human legs being significantly longer, he got there first. He knelt down. The coil looked heavy, and he reminded himself of some advice Owen had given him: *Lift with your legs, not with your back.*

He wedged his left hand under the outside of the coil and reached in toward the dark well at its center with his right.

HISSSS!

Daffy leapt across the deck and landed atop the coil, hissing madly.

Henry was so surprised by the sudden assault that he fell backward, landing on the deck. He looked down and saw three thin red lines along the back of his right hand.

"She scratched me!" he blurted, and as he looked up, he saw that Daffy wasn't done scratching yet. She was perched on the top of the coil, batting down into the circular hollow at its center with both front paws, like a tiny, clawed boxer.

"Must be a rat in there," said Aaron, looming over Henry

and reaching down to help him to his feet. "You're lucky you didn't stick your hand inside."

Henry nodded, imagining how much worse his wound would have been if it had come from a rat's teeth. But as he rose back to his feet and peered inside the coil, he got a glimpse of the horrible truth.

He gasped and took a quick step back. "That's no rat," he breathed. "Not anymore."

"Oh, dear Lord," said Aaron, seeing it now too.

Poking out of the coiled rope was the face of a rat, slick with clear slime and baring two long blackened teeth at the cat just above it. But the head around its face was covered in dark red armor and topped with two bobbing antennas. Daffy tagged one of them with her paw, sending it waving wildly back and forth. The rat creature hissed loudly and rose to its full height. Its two front legs appeared in the sunlight, and then two middle legs. Each of them ended not in claws but in barbs.

Emma appeared at a run, her sister's spear gripped tightly in her right hand. "Daffy, get out of there!" she shouted. The ship's cat paid her no mind, bunching up her hind legs and preparing to pounce down on the thing in the rope.

"*Ay, Dios mío*," Henry heard her breathe, and then a moment before the cat leapt, Emma did.

She landed on the opposite side of the coil from Daffy, and as she did, she drove the spear down hard.

The iron spike found a home in the rat-creature's back. Henry heard a thick crunch as it penetrated the hard exoskeleton.

Daffy made a *mer!* sound and leapt in the other direction, away from the sudden impact.

Emma twisted the iron point in deeper, pinning the thing to the wood of the deck.

Henry took a few steps forward and peered down inside the coil. He watched the bizarre creature squirm and twitch and then, a few moments later, fall still. He stared down at its body, more insect than rat now and covered with the same slime they'd seen before.

"Where did it come from?" said Aaron.

Henry remembered the rustling tarp, just minutes earlier. "From below," he said.

Suddenly, he saw movement within the coil. A little puff of white dust floated free of the creature's mouth, and then another. More white powder drifted upward from the hole in its back. Henry's eyes grew wide with both recognition and fear.

"Get back!" he said, and when Aaron and Emma continued to stare down at the little carcass, he yelled it. "GET BACK!"

He turned and all but wrestled them the first few steps, until they turned and began moving on their own. Finally, when they were a good ten feet away, he released them and turned to see which way the wind was blowing.

He saw the spear sticking straight up out of the center of the coil and a small white cloud rising from inside. But as soon as the tiny particles cleared the top of the rope, the stiff sea breeze carried them through the rope railing and out to sea.

Henry released the breath he'd been holding.

"What was that cloud?" said Emma.

"Those were spores," he said. "Fungal spores."

"And, uh, what are those?" asked Aaron.

"It's how they reproduce," he said.

"Oh!" said Emma. "You mean . . ."

Henry nodded. "It's what that rat must have breathed in, and Obed before it."

"And Wrickitts before them both," said Owen from just behind them.

The others had left their tasks now and headed over to see what the commotion was about. Thacher moved around the little group, angling for a better look.

"Don't go near it," said Henry. "Not just yet."

"Are you going to tell us what happened, at least?" said Thacher.

"Henry was saved by a girl," said Aaron.

Henry just nodded. He didn't find that embarrassing in the least.

"And a cat," he added.

CHAPTER 26

LAND HO!

Henry gazed at the rat-creature's remains through the walls of a clear glass jar. Checking once again to make sure that the lid was secured tightly, he carefully turned the jar around in his hands. He felt the weight of the little monster within shift and tumble. The inside of the glass was lightly frosted with fine white spores. He gazed through them into the creature's open mouth. He saw the small tongue inside, a tiny slip of fuzzy whiteness. He noted a few more details: the blackened teeth, the exoskeleton . . .

There was no doubt it had been transformed by the same fungus. *Remarkable*, he thought. *It infected an entirely different species . . .*

He was alone in the cabin now, alone with his thoughts.

The species was more adaptable—and more contagious—than he had feared.

His master's legacy was a voracious and opportunistic predator.

These troubling thoughts were cut short by an excited cry from out on deck. *Did I hear that right?* he wondered. But the same call came again. He carefully wrapped the jar in a scrap of blanket and stowed it in his trunk. He locked it tight and then rushed out on deck.

As soon as he emerged from the door, the call came a third time. It was Emma's voice, carrying down from high up in the rigging. "Land ho!" she called, and then, pausing just long enough to gather more breath, she called again. "Land ho!"

"Are you certain?" Aaron called up from his place at the helm.

Emma leaned out from the foremast crosstrees. Her weight far forward, it was only her extraordinary balance that kept her from toppling out of her perch and splattering onto the deck below. She squinted into the distance, and there it was.

It wasn't much more than a fuzzy line rising along the center of the horizon now, but she was sure. She had seen that fuzzy line before—or fuzzy lines like it, anyway. The color was darker than the water below it, a green-black rising from a world of blue. It was land, all right, and a lot of it.

She leaned back slightly and called down once more: "Yes, it's land!"

"I'll get the spyglass!" called Owen, who now carried a compass in his vest pocket instead.

Emma swung down from the crow's nest and began descending the rigging. She had been placed up there as a lookout, and she had done her job. They'd known from the charts that they were approaching Cuba. They'd even spotted a few more sails off in the distance, as they approached the busy island. They'd been going too slowly to overtake any of those ships, and instead they'd kept their eyes out for the western edge of Cuba.

As Emma neared the deck, she knew there was a problem. And as Owen returned from the cabin, already extending the spyglass, she knew what he'd see. Cuba was dead ahead.

They'd found it—but they'd found too much of it. She hadn't spotted the western edge of the island off to starboard. She'd spotted the whole darn thing looming up in front of them. And she knew what that meant.

She watched Owen closely as she dropped lightly down to the deck and took up her usual post beside her sister. He peered through the glass, first straight ahead and then, very slowly, from side to side. He repeated the motions exactly and then deflated utterly. His shoulders slumped, and his chin dropped as he lowered the glass from his eye.

Thacher snatched it away, and Owen let him.

"Something went wrong," he said, his voice soft and distant. He looked up and met Emma's eyes. She saw his confusion, saw him redoing some calculation or other in his head.

"It's not your fault," she said, and she truly meant it. Anything could have gone wrong. The calculations could have been a little off, or the currents. The steering could have drifted a few extra points since they took their last bearings. Everyone was tired and scared. And then, of course, there was the matter of Thacher ransacking the maps. That Owen, a novice navigator, had managed to guide them all this way and get them so close seemed a marvel to her. The others seemed to agree.

"There it is!" hollered Thacher.

"Where? Where? Let me see!" pleaded Aaron.

"Hand it over, boys, I'll have a look," said Maria.

But Emma knew Owen was in no mood to celebrate a near miss. The plan had been to skirt past the edge of the island and then continue the short distance to the Florida territory. But they had missed and were heading directly toward the middle of Cuba, which Spain ruled with an iron hand.

She wondered what he would do next. It was no idle question. In many ways, their entire future—if they were to have one—depended on it. You can't sail through an island, she knew, only to it or around it.

Suddenly, the spyglass was thrust into her hands. Everyone else had had a turn, and now it was hers.

The view through the glass was much the same as the one she'd had aloft. The fuzzy line became a fuzzy lump. And as the ship lumbered on, the line grew, not just taller but also wider.

"We are striking it amidships!" crowed Thacher. "We could hardly miss it now."

Owen roughly snatched the glass back from Emma's hands and slapped it closed. "But miss it we will," he said loudly.

She turned to look at him. She understood this for what it was: not rudeness but a show of force, a demonstration of will.

"What do you mean?" said Thacher. "You can't possibly be saying . . ." Still staring incredulously at Owen, he pointed straight ahead. "It is right there. *Right. There.*"

"But that is *not* where we are *going*," Owen growled back. He stared back at Thacher for a few long seconds. Then he looked around at the whole group, save for Aaron, who had retreated back to the wheel.

"We will sail around the island and continue to Florida as planned," he said.

Eyes gazed back at him in disbelief. Mouths dropped open in astonishment. They had all seen enough maps to know that Cuba was a huge island. Sailing around it would add days to their journey. Her thoughts swirled. They'd had a plan, and she'd agreed with it. But now? The plan had failed, but in its failure it had delivered them to the very edge of land . . .

And was it a coincidence or divine providence that it had happened on the same day that a new sort of monster had been discovered? And it was a new threat that could prove even worse than the boy-faced horror below. Because sailing ships, as she knew from bitter experience, were *full* of rats. She remembered the worst nights, when she'd been forced to go to sleep with her boots on to keep the rats from gnawing at her feet.

Owen turned on his heel and barked an order to the wheel. "Hard to port, Aaron!"

Aaron blinked back at him, and then responded, "Are you joking?"

"I most certainly am not!" Owen boomed. "You will turn this ship or I will!"

He took two long forceful strides back toward the wheel. Aaron's eyes grew wide, and he began turning hard. Owen slowed and then stopped as a hand slapped down on his right shoulder. It was Thacher's.

Uh-oh, thought Emma.

Owen spun around, his left hand reaching round to peel Thacher's hand free and his right hand reaching for his belt.

Emma gasped as Owen gripped his pistol.

Thacher released his shoulder and backed away.

All eyes were on Owen's right hand. It was only when he followed their gazes that he realized what he'd done—or at least that's the way it seemed to Emma. Whatever the case, he quickly dropped his hand from his gun.

The shipped bucked on the waves as it began its abrupt turn to the left, and the assembled crew members sank low to keep their balance. Emma reached over to help her sister, stealing a quick look at her bandaged foot. It looked like a packet that had fallen off the butcher's wagon and into the street. Maria's balance was solid, even on one good leg, and her shoulder felt warm and reassuring under Emma's palm. Maria acknowledged the help with a quick nod. Henry, of course, fell down, banging one knee on the deck. "Ow!" he said.

"Careful there," said Owen. The little distraction seemed to lower the tension slightly. Emma's eyes darted upward instinctively to see how the wind was hitting the sails as their direction shifted.

"We'll need to adjust the sheets and stays," she said.

The others shot their own quick looks up at the flapping canvas. "We will," said Thacher, "*if* we are to go through with this ludicrous change of course."

Emma didn't know what "ludicrous" meant, but from the way Owen visibly bristled at the sound of it, she knew it wasn't good.

"What do you mean 'if'?" said Owen.

"I mean that this affects all of us," said Thacher, narrowing his eyes like a cat on the hunt. "And as such, we all deserve a say. I demand a meeting, a vote." He waved his hand around in an abrupt circle, nearly slapping Henry's face. "We all do!"

"Huh?" said Henry.

Emma was equally surprised to find herself included, but her sister wasn't. "It's only fair," said Maria, before elbowing Emma not especially lightly in the side.

"Oof," said Emma. She wasn't sure she agreed, but she didn't want another of her sister's sharp elbows. "A meeting couldn't hurt," she said, instantly regretting her choice of words. Hadn't this all begun with a meeting on deck one stormy night?

She said the words without conviction, but they hit Owen like a cannonball at the waterline. She risked a quick look over and saw the expression that flashed across his face, that particular combination of hurt and surprise that meant one thing: betrayal. "I didn't mean . . ." she mumbled.

"What are you all talking about?" Aaron called up from the wheel.

"A meeting!" Maria called back.

Aaron smiled widely. "Should I keep turning, then?"

Owen looked up from his dark thoughts. "Hold this course for now," he called.

"We'll have the meeting?" said Thacher.

Owen nodded. His body was tense and drawn in, like that of an animal being hunted. Emma knew he felt outnumbered and wanted to remind him that the votes had not yet been cast. She couldn't, though, because she still had no idea how she would vote.

"Yes, we'll meet," said Owen. His eyes scanned the deck, and she knew he was thinking of that first meeting too. "But not out here. Not again."

The crew filed into the captain's cabin once more.

"You stay at the helm," Owen said to Aaron, who was still steering his compromise course, neither straight toward the island nor entirely past it. "We all know your vote well enough."

It wasn't until the cabin door swung shut behind them that Emma realized the full weight of those words. Thacher, Maria, and Aaron had long been for the nearest land. Owen and Henry seemed just as determined to make landfall in the United States.

And that left only her.

She could create a tie, or break one.

A tie could get ugly but so could landfall in Cuba. And yet she would have to decide, not just for her, but for all of them.

CHAPTER 27

A VOTE, INTERRUPTED

Emma took her place at the small table. There was barely enough space for the five of them, and too few chairs, but they made do with a trunk here and a stool there.

"You all know where I stand," Owen said as soon as everyone was seated. For a moment it seemed like that was all he'd say, but his pride had been hurt and he couldn't resist one last chance to try to make his case. "This is a United States ship, and we must take it back to a port where those laws, and rights, will be protected. The Spanish? They take everything and send it back to Spain. The *Polaris* will be sailing under a new name and a Spanish flag within the week, and we will be lucky not to be working in the cane fields."

"Ridiculous," said Thacher. "The Spanish are no enemies of ours. And what do I care who owns this ship—it certainly won't be me! And do not threaten me with forced labor. Am I not already indentured? No, I have suffered enough on this voyage. *We have all* suffered enough on this voyage. Let us make haste to port and let Spanish rifles and torches kill this horrible thing we carry with us, before it kills us!"

Maria agreed: "Yes, Spanish rifles and a Cuban doctor, and beyond that, things will be fine." She looked over at Emma, sitting next to her at the little table. "We speak Spanish, remember, nor have we thrown out our headscarves and wraps. Many ships sail from Havana each day, and all need ship's boys, especially ones with experience. We will all be sailing again within the week!"

Emma resented being spoken for. She was close to her sister, but she was her own person too. And the idea of dressing up and playing boy once again held no appeal for her. The sight of Obed's face on a monster's body had made up her mind. From the first time she'd seen it, she'd thought, *It is a wicked thing to be forced to be something other than yourself.*

She opened her mouth to speak, but as she struggled to choose her first words, Henry cut in. His vote was expected, but his reason for it caught everyone off guard.

"We have a responsibility to science," he said. The others, regardless of allegiance looked around at each other. Emma looked at her sister, Owen looked at Thacher, and their eyes all said the same thing: *Really? To science?* Perhaps sensing the skepticism, Henry raised his voice. "The creature lurking between decks, or creatures"—he cast a glance over at his trunk in the corner—"they are monstrous, to be sure, but they are also marvels. It is a species entirely unknown to science and capable of remarkable feats of transformation and adaptation. The capture and study of this species could lead to tremendous benefits—"

Thacher cut in: "This is a creature that has *absorbed* my friend, a creature that you yourself said would try to do the same to us . . ."

Henry shrugged weakly. "I said it was monstrous."

Emma stared at Thacher. She hadn't realized that he had been friends with Obed, though it made some sense, now that she thought about it. They were both such bitter boys, badly served by their lives.

Henry rallied: "This voyage—the voyage you all signed on for—was a scientific expedition. This species *is* that science! It is the fruit of our labor." He turned to Owen. "And the labor of those who have been lost. And it is a grand discovery. If we reach the United States, it will be considered a wonder. The museums and benefactors and the government itself, who have together funded the trip, will get their money's worth. As for us, we will, I dare say, have done our part for both science and history."

"Oh, yes, yes," said Thacher. "It will be quite historic when we sail into port with our faces bobbing about on slimy insect bodies."

"He is right, though—it was a scientific expedition," said Owen.

"*Is* a scientific expedition," corrected Henry.

"It is an experiment in everything that can go wrong aboard a boat!" said Maria.

"Enough bickering!" shouted Thacher, as if he hadn't started it in the first place. "The vote stands at three to two, and there is only one vote remaining."

Around the table, all eyes turned to Emma. She swallowed nervously, but then she straightened up. She was as much a member of this crew as anyone. She wasn't even sure the ship would still be afloat if it wasn't for her. The others seemed to feel at least some of that too, as they waited in silence for her vote. She looked up at them, cleared her throat with a bit more confidence, and began to speak.

"If I had loved Spain, I would not have left it," she said, opening with a simple statement of fact before trying to mine her feelings further. "To be a poor and parentless girl in any nation is to know its soul." She paused, quite proud of herself for forming such a fine phrase in English.

"I did not come in here to listen to political theories," groused Thacher. She cut him off with a glare, and he shut his mouth and looked away, not wanting to antagonize her before her vote.

"And Spain, though I think it has not always been . . . but . . . now . . ." Suddenly, her English had grown elusive again. "She is a *glotón*. You understand?"

"A glutton," said Henry. "Greedy."

"*Sí*—yes," said Emma. She opened her mouth and raised one finger so that no one would cut her off as she searched for the right words. For the Spain she knew *was* greedy. She had been at the docks, hungry and looking for work, as the overworked crews offloaded heaping piles of gold, silver, and sugar from the empire's far-flung colonies. All that wealth, and where did it go? Not to the people, not to the orphans left starving in the streets. It made her so angry, but there was no one to complain to—and she knew how ruthlessly the crown put down any challenges to its authority at home. She had heard it did far, far worse out in those lucrative colonies. She glanced out the bank of windows and corrected herself: out in *these* lucrative colonies.

How could she trust her fate to such an authority, and in such a place? She looked over at her sister. Maria was confident that they'd be allowed to go on their way and find work on the next ship. But Maria, she was reasonably sure, was wrong. More likely they would be pressed into grim service: slaves to the crown, if not in name then in practice. And that was if they could continue to pass as boys. *How long can that go on? And where will it end?* She hardly dared consider. Then again, her sister's wounded foot seemed to get worse each day . . .

But the moment had stretched out too long now. Her open mouth was in danger of catching flies, and the others were growing impatient. Thacher shifted loudly in his chair. Owen cleared his throat.

"I have made up my mind," Emma blurted, hoping that saying it would make it so.

The others leaned in around the little table.

But the next sound was not that of Emma's decisive vote, it was a sudden crash and the sound of splintering wood.

"What was that?" said Thacher.

"Could it be the mast again?" said Maria. "Have we sprung another yard?"

Emma looked at her. She was disappointed that her sister would play along in this awful game, but she understood it down to her bones. It was a simple, human desire for self-preservation. Somehow it made Emma like them all a little more even as it made her hate them all a little bit. The cabin walls were thick, the door was closed, and they were all huddled together inside, along with oversized Owen and his gun. It would be so easy to stay this way, to hunker down.

Except they weren't *all* huddled together inside.

Sickened by this conspiracy of inaction, even as she took part in it, Emma finally managed to say the word they were all thinking. "Aaron," she breathed.

And then it was as if she'd broken a spell. They rose as one, even Maria on her tender foot. Emma unsheathed the first of her two knives as the others pulled their own weapons from their belts or grabbed one of the spares that now lined the cabin. "That was no sprung yard," said Owen. "Come on!"

Emma met his eyes. Had he said that just a few moments earlier she would have been so proud of him. As it was, they didn't even make it to the door before they heard the scream. It was an awful thing. High-pitched and ragged, it cut through the walls of the cabin, speaking of both pain and fear.

Owen flung the door open, already pointing the pistol out into the sunlight as he rushed onto the deck. Thacher crowded out next. Then Emma and Henry, bumping shoulders as they pressed through the narrow door.

"There!" said Henry, pointing toward the aft hatch.

The boards that had been nailed over it were shattered and scattered. And disappearing back down the dark hole at its center was the creature's bulbous, dark red abdomen and the last of its six legs.

And then Emma saw something else, something she wished she hadn't. It was a hand, *Aaron's* hand. It reached back around the creature's hulking body and grabbed the edge of one side of the hatch.

There was a sharp crack and a quick sizzling as the flintlock ignited its charge.

Per-KRACK! went the pistol. A flash of flame and a billowing plume of smoke shot forth.

The ball struck what she could only think of as the fat red balloon at the tail end of the beast, producing a quick puff of white powder. What had Henry called them? *The spores?* The thing was lined with them. She covered her mouth and nose but kept her eyes wide open.

And so she saw Aaron's feeble grip torn from the hatchway as the creature disappeared, quick as the flick of a tongue, down into the dark belly of the ship.

The sea breeze quickly dispersed both the gun smoke and the floating spores, carrying them over the rail as it thinned them into invisibility. She lowered her hand from her mouth. The air she sucked in smelled as sulfurous and hot as the devil's own domain.

"It took him," said Henry.

His voice was thick with sadness, but Thacher turned on him anyway.

"What was it you said?" he snarled. "We have *a responsibility to science*?" He swung around, waving his hatchet so wildly that it seemed certain to chop into one of them. Instead, he pointed it down the dark, torn hole of the aft hatch. "Well, it seems that science feels no responsibility to us!"

Beside them, Owen rushed back into the cabin to reload. "I have wounded it," he said as he reached the door. "I have shot it in its monstrous rear!"

And then he disappeared inside and they were left with nothing but some sharpened steel between them and a gaping hole in the deck.

Thacher swung back around, once again almost clipping Henry with the gleaming blade of his hatchet. "Well," he said. "What do you have to say about that?"

Henry blinked at him, as if waking from a dream. "It was waiting," he whispered.

"What's that?" said Thacher, who honestly seemed not to have heard.

"It was waiting for one of us to be alone," said Henry, louder this time.

Thacher seemed taken aback. He lowered his hatchet, and Emma let out the breath she'd been holding. "Is it truly that . . . intelligent?"

Henry nodded, and then all of them turned to look at the gaping hole in the deck.

"It is wounded now," said Maria, holding on to the railing to take the weight off her own wound.

Henry shook his head. "A nuisance to it, at best," he said. "It was not a vital area, and it will not feel pain as we do."

Emma scowled at him. "Will you ever have any good news?"

Suddenly, Owen reappeared, causing them all to jump.

"Gah! Do not sneak up on us like that!" snapped Maria. "Not now."

"Sorry," said Owen, speaking to Maria but staring straight down into the open hatchway.

Emma admired his focus. It seemed entirely appropriate.

But it was also why he never saw Thacher swing the hatchet.

CHAPTER 28

AS GOOD AS DEAD

Owen woke up with a splitting headache and a bigger question looming: Was his head, in fact, split? He raised his hand slowly toward his scalp, afraid his fingers would find it slick with blood. He groaned miserably and didn't dare open his eyes. He could feel the sun on his face and didn't think he could handle all that light just yet.

His fingers delicately probed the back of his head. What he found there wasn't the clotted mess he had feared but instead a lump the size of half an egg. He winced and sucked in air through his teeth as his fingers brushed the tender, taut skin.

Still not ready for the sunlight, he tried to slow his breathing and listen. *I can hardly hear anything over this hammering in my head*, he thought groggily. But a moment later, as some of the fog parted in his battered brain, he realized that the hammering wasn't in his head at all.

His eyes snapped open.

"Ugh," he groaned, but as his eyes grew accustomed to the light, the fog lifted a bit more.

The image in front of him shimmered and shifted in ways it

shouldn't have, but he could still see what was happening. Emma and Henry were on their knees around the aft hatch, nailing bits of board, scraps of wood, and what looked to be the remains of a chair over the top of it.

Thacher was standing above them with a pistol—with *Owen's* pistol.

"You scum!" said Owen, his voice coming out dry and raspy. He tried to rise to his feet, but dizziness hit him like a rogue wave and he immediately sank back down to the deck.

The hammering stopped as Thacher and the others turned toward him.

"Let them go," Owen growled at Thacher.

Thacher stared at him, briefly baffled, and then broke into a broad smile. "Oh, what? You think I am forcing them to board up this hatch *at gunpoint*?" He laughed with a genuine good humor that Owen instantly hated. "I don't think I could stop them." He waved the pistol around in the air, making a show of not pointing it at the others. "I am *guarding* them as they work."

Owen looked at the other two again. Emma mouthed the word "sorry" while Henry gawked back at him, hammer still suspended midswing.

"Oh," said Owen. That did make more sense now that he thought about it. Still, he was angry and searched his foggy brain for some words to lash out with. "Boards are useless," he spat. It was the best he had.

"We fastened some of the iron spikes underneath," said Emma, with an odd brightness. "And left lots of nails sticking out of the bottom."

"Like an upside-down porcupine," added Henry.

Owen stared at him. "But . . . Aaron . . ." He couldn't quite find the words in his foggy state, but it seemed very clear to him. The creature had captured their crew mate and now they were sealing him down there with it.

He saw the others exchange quick, pained glances. *They've talked about this,* he realized.

"Aaron is dead," said Thacher.

"Do you know that?" said Owen.

Henry took his turn: "Dead, or as good as dead."

It took Owen a few moments to realize Henry was talking about the infection and the grim transformation it led to. He felt a sudden rush of emotion for the cautious boy. He imagined Aaron, frozen in horror at the wheel, as the beast ripped through the hatch. A tear ran down his face before he even realized it had formed.

"Perhaps you should rest for a bit," said Thacher.

"REST?" blurted Owen, the sudden volume releasing a lightning bolt of pain along his scalp. He pushed on, a bit more quietly. "I am lucky to be alive!"

"Oh, don't be a baby," said Thacher. His annoyingly good mood had vanished with the talk of Aaron, but now it returned. "I hit you with the blunt side."

Owen processed that for a moment: *Struck with the blunt side of a hatchet* . . . "Please don't do me any more favors," he said, managing to lean forward.

"Don't worry," said Thacher, a devilish smile sliding onto his face. "This will all be over soon."

"What do you . . ." Owen began, but then he did the math. Where was Maria? He swung his head back around toward the helm. His senses reeled from the sudden movement, but as soon as the stars cleared from his vision, he saw her there at the wheel. He turned his head forward again. He couldn't see above the bow, but he knew that she was steering straight for the Cuban coast.

He sat there helplessly for a few moments, taking in what he could see. The pistol in Thacher's hand, the hatchet back in his belt. Emma and Henry, giving him one last concerned look before going back to their equally concerned hammering. He looked at their makeshift hatch cover, a thick mass of mismatched wood that resembled a poorly made raft.

This is what a mutiny looks like, he thought. *It's all the ordinary things and familiar faces, but arranged in a completely unexpected way.* He shook his sore head slowly, trying to clear a few more cobwebs. He took a few deep breaths. That worked better.

Well, whatever it looks like, he decided, *I will have to put a stop to it.*

He bit his lower lip, pulled his wobbly legs underneath him, and rose slowly to his feet.

CHAPTER 29

LEAVE A STRAIGHT WAKE

Owen hauled himself across the deck toward Thacher. The others stopped hammering as they turned to watch the confrontation. Thacher took a few steps back as the larger boy approached. But Owen was moving unsteadily, dragging his feet heavily across the wood and nearly toppling over with each modest rise and fall of the deck. He squinted into the bright sunlight and kept his left hand on his wounded head.

Seeing this, Thacher relaxed. "Now, settle down," he said. "I don't want to hurt you again. The decision has been made and . . ." He hesitated, considering the wisdom of his next words, but then he said them anyway. "And enough people have died aboard this ship. We are taking her in."

Owen kept coming, one wobbly step at a time. Thacher cast a quick, uncertain look down toward the pistol, confirming Owen's suspicion that he had never actually fired one before. Owen drew within five feet of him, then four, then three . . .

"I am warning you," said Thacher, taking half a step back and raising the pistol slightly.

Owen stopped just short of the raised barrel, swaying on his feet like a sleepwalker.

"*Thacherrrr,*" said Emma, drawing his name out in warning.

Thacher took one more look at his woozy opponent and then risked a quick look over at Emma. "What am I supposed—"

And just like that, quick as a rattlesnake, Owen's right hand flashed up and out, slapping the pistol away. With the barrel pointing somewhere out to sea, Thacher squeezed the trigger on pure reflex—but he hadn't pulled back the hammer. He looked down, suddenly realizing his mistake. Both of Owen's strong hands were on the gun now. Thacher rushed to bring his left across, but it was too late.

Using the barrel as leverage, Owen twisted the pistol easily from his grasp. He flipped it around skillfully, bringing the flint back as part of the same fluid motion.

"But how?" Thacher gasped, staring down at the pistol, which was now pointed at his midsection. "You can barely even walk."

"Can't I?" said Owen, doing a quick little jig step.

"That was all an *act*?" said Emma. "I was worried about you!"

Owen answered her without taking his eyes off Thacher. "Oh, my head *definitely* hurts—not faking that—but I'm moving just fine."

Thacher cast another glance down, this time toward the hatchet at his belt.

"*Thacherrrr*," said Owen, imitating Emma's warning tone. "Kindly toss that overboard."

"But you will leave me unarmed," he protested.

"Aye," said Owen, "that is my intention."

Thacher slowly pulled the hatchet from his belt and tossed it over the improvised rope railing. Its splash was lost in the ship's wake, but with Thacher disarmed, the tension seemed to bleed away from the deck.

"If you must hold on to something," said Owen, "grab a hammer and finish nailing up that hatchway."

Thacher gave him a long, hard look. "You're a fool," he grumbled, but then he took the hammer from Henry and got to work, angrily battering home the last few nails.

Owen carefully uncocked the pistol and slipped it back into his belt. Then he turned and headed for the wheel. "I'll take that too," he said to Maria.

Maria watched his steady approach. There was no wobble to his walk now. "I would prefer to stay at the wheel for now," she said as he got closer. "It is just about the only thing holding me up."

Owen looked down at her bandaged foot. The wrapping was ragged and discolored, and the foot itself was swollen almost as round as an orange. *She'll be lucky if they don't have to cut that off*, he thought. And as he looked up and caught her eyes, he knew that she was thinking the same thing.

"Fair enough," he said. "You do the steering."

Maria cocked her head slightly, not sure she understood him. "And *where* should I steer?" she said.

Owen turned back around and looked out over the bow. Land was much closer now, the approaching island visible without his scope. A cool ocean breeze at their back pushed the waterlogged ship onward and fingered through his hair, soothing the bruised lump underneath. He looked up and saw a little convoy of shorebirds flapping and darting above the mastheads.

The last of the hammering stopped, the patched aft hatch as secure as it was going to get. Owen sized it up. The creature had torn through the hatch like silk before, and he couldn't imagine a few downward-facing spikes would make much difference. He raised his eyes to the forward hatch, still no more secure than the aft one had been.

The monster is uncontained and uncontrolled, governed only by its own unknowable motives.

"Owen?" said Maria.

"A moment, please," he said, still watching the horizon.

Now the eyes of the others turned toward him as well. They had expected him to bring the ship hard to port, to resume sailing around the island. *He* had expected to bring the ship hard to port. But now, as the shorebirds called down to the deck, inquiring about any chance of food, he realized that he was not quite ready to make that decision.

So much had happened that day, and now Owen paused to consider it all. He had been challenged by Thacher, but he had won. He had been wronged, and he had prevailed. And of course, he had the gun back. He was fully in charge, he now realized, for the first time. And it was about time he was fully honest with himself as well.

He'd considered himself in charge before: next man up for the post of captain. But it wasn't true. He wasn't the captain. He wasn't even a junior captain in charge of a junior crew. He was a cabin boy—a good one, it was true, but still just a cabin boy. A cabin boy playing at being captain—a title that took a lifetime at sea to earn.

He looked over at the others.

Emma: a better sailor than him.

Maria: braver than him and with, no doubt, far more tolerance for pain.

Henry: an abysmal sailor but as smart as anyone he'd ever met.

And finally, he looked at Thacher, who looked down to avoid his stare. Thacher, the pain in the butt. Thacher, the sneaky such-and-such. Thacher, bitter and dark . . . Finally, Thacher looked up and met his eyes.

Thacher, who had been right all along.

The revelation rocked Owen where he stood. He could not risk the few remaining lives on board for one moment longer than necessary. Not for pride, and not for profit.

"Owen?" said Maria, breaking in on his tumultuous thoughts. "Which way?"

Owen cleared his throat, just to buy himself another moment. Was he sure about this? But the next words he spoke were loud and clear.

"Take her in, Maria," he said, turning back toward the wheel. "Make for land, and leave a straight wake."

Maria smiled, a big toothy smile that made Owen smile back despite himself. "Are you sure?" she said.

"Funny," he said. "I was just asking myself the same thing. But I am sure." He looked back toward the others, seeking out Henry, in particular. "Unless there are any objections?"

Henry had backed away from the patched-up hatch, and the question seemed to rouse him from his own heavy thoughts. "No," he said, shaking his head firmly. "We cannot release this pestilence upon an unsuspecting land. It is not only more contagious than I thought, but it is smarter as well. It would spread like a wildfire."

"And what of our responsibility to science?" said Thacher from the far rail. Owen didn't blame him for seeking to soothe his own wounded pride.

242

"It is true that we have an obligation to science—that I have an obligation to science," said Henry. "I did not misspeak, but I can see now that science itself must be exercised responsibly. And besides," he added cryptically, "there may be another way to satisfy that responsibility."

Owen was about to ask him what that might be, but Henry kept talking, his tone turning darker. "But there is a problem," he said. "This organism is contained deep within this ship. It is impossible to say what forms it might have taken by now, be it boy or rat. It may even be growing in the very walls."

Owen nodded solemnly. "We will have to destroy the ship." He could hardly believe his own words, but at the same time, he knew they were true.

Henry gave him a curious look. "Yes, but that is not the problem."

Owen blinked back at him, incredulous. What could be worse than destroying this noble ship, the fruit of his own family's labors?

Henry clarified. "The fungus is contained within the ship," he said. "But we have all seen the deadly white spores . . ." He allowed his words to trail off, as if the implication was clear.

The others looked around at each other, not yet comprehending.

Finally, Thacher spoke up on their behalf: "So? I'm afraid I don't follow."

Henry looked at him, as if trying to decide if the other boy was being serious. He shook his head and took a deep breath. He exhaled slowly and then pronounced his grim verdict. "The fungus is contained deep within the ship," he repeated. "But it could also be contained in any one of us."

CHAPTER 30

A SPORE SUBJECT

Henry stood his ground on deck and did his best to field the barrage of questions that followed.

"What do you mean, infected?" barked Owen.

"I mean, um, infected," said Henry.

"I feel quite human, thank you!" said Thacher.

"Well, you would, I think, at least at first . . ."

"I mean, sure, I haven't washed in a while," protested Emma, "but I don't think I am *a fungus*."

"It doesn't work like, I mean, it gets inside the host," said Henry, rushing to explain before he was cut off again. "Affects the brain first, I think, makes you clumsy. I've read of it in insects . . ."

"Yes, yes, and seen it in Wrickitts," said Owen. "And in the trembling walk of the Obed beast—but you're the one who falls over all the time!"

"And she's the one with a limp!" said Thacher, pointing at Maria at the wheel.

"Aah!" said Maria, indignant. "That is only because my foot is infected."

"Exactly!" said Thacher, taking a quick step away from her.

Henry knew he needed to put a stop to this quickly. A little suspicion, in the absence of reliable information, could be a very dangerous thing.

"It could be ANY OF US!" he yelled. "Or all of us—or none of us!"

"But you said . . ." said Thacher.

"Yes, yes, the walk, and then a rash, a perfumy smell," said Henry, frustrated. "We know the symptoms, but not how long it takes them to start to show. Wrickitts made it all the way back from the jungle, remember."

"You are saying we could have this thing inside of us and not know it," said Owen, clearly wrestling with the idea. "And not even show it?"

"And not show it *yet*," said Henry.

"A mushroom does not grow overnight," added Emma.

"Exactly!" said Henry, relieved that someone else understood.

"I truly hope I am not a mushroom," she added softly.

"But how can we know?" said Thacher. "We can't just . . . wait?"

And for that, Henry had no answer. "Uhhhh . . ." He tried to think of what Dr. Wetherby would have done. A quarantine, perhaps, a waiting period, keeping a close watch for any signs. Perhaps he would have them attempt to walk a straight line? He looked up to find everyone staring back at him, still waiting on an answer he didn't have.

"Perhaps if we waited a few—"

"No!" said Thacher. "We have waited enough. We are in mortal danger here. We will reach the shore before nightfall, and I am not spending another night upon this accursed vessel."

Henry stared back at him. "You would bring this thing with you?"

"I told you, I feel fine!" he said.

"Me too," said Emma.

"Quite hearty," said Owen.

"My foot hurts, is all."

"But . . ." Hadn't he just explained this to them? "We cannot. Not until we know for sure."

He surveyed their deeply doubtful expressions. He needed to make them understand. "This is a thinking organism: versatile and highly adaptive. It is a danger to civilization itself!"

"It is a sneaky devil," conceded Owen.

"Well," said Emma, looking around the circle. "How long would we have to wait?"

"I am *not* waiting!" said Thacher.

Maria gazed up into the sky. At first Henry thought she was looking at the sails, but then he realized she was looking beyond them, toward the heavens. She whispered a quick prayer in

Spanish and then dropped her head and said, "This is a test. Surely, we are being tested."

The words hit Henry like a lightning bolt. "What did you say?"

"I said we are being tested."

Henry's expression brightened and he broke into a broad smile. *Of course*, he thought. *That is exactly what Wetherby would have done. Perhaps the scope?* He remembered the fuzzy white tongues of both creatures. *Yes, that could work.*

"Why are you smiling?" said Maria.

"What are you up to?" said Thacher.

He ignored the questions and looked at the wheel in Maria's hands. "Can we tie that off?" he said. "I will need everyone in the cabin." He paused. "And we do *not* want to leave anyone out here alone this time."

"Everyone in the cabin?" said Owen. "For what?"

Henry turned and looked him in the eyes, the smile falling from his face as he got down to business. "Why, for the test, of course."

CHAPTER 31

TRIAL BY SCIENCE

Emma filed into the captain's cabin with the rest of them.

"Do you need any help?" she asked her sister, but Maria shook her off and limped in with her pride intact.

Emma sought out her eyes—*how are you?*—but Maria kept her gaze down toward the floor. Emma moved on to the next pressing topic: *How am I?*

She felt her pulse thrumming in her veins. She was nervous. She *had* seen the deathly spores, and up close too. She remembered bringing the spear down on the rat-thing. She remembered the puff that had escaped from within its strange armor.

The blood pushed through her veins faster. Were those tiny spores inside her? She'd seen them so clearly, been so close. In all that gusting wind, had she breathed them too? *Oh God*, she thought. *What if it's me?*

She kept those thoughts to herself and did her best to appear calm. She looked around at the others, but none of them met her eyes. *Are they all thinking the same thing?*

"Should we all sit at the table?" asked Thacher.

Henry was already kneeling over his leather trunk. "Sit where you like," he said, unlocking it and popping open the latches. "But we will need to do this one at a time."

He opened the trunk and began pawing around inside. First he pulled out a book and then a strange metal-and-glass contraption that looked like nothing Emma had ever seen before. He walked over to the head of the little table and set them down. Then he pulled out a chair for himself and began flipping through the book.

From the other corner of the table, Emma raised up on her tiptoes to get a look at the pages. In the light streaming in through the back windows, she saw pages of heavy black text alternating with pages of precise, detailed illustrations.

"Here it is," said Henry. "'Chapter Thirty: Fungal Spores.'"

"Sounds fascinating," said Thacher sarcastically.

"I assure you," said Henry, flipping to a page of illustrations, "it is very compelling."

"Well," admitted Owen, "you certainly have our attention now."

"Good," said Henry. "Then we'll begin. Owen, could you turn the lamp up, please."

"How high?" said Owen, reaching out for the lamp as it swung lightly from its perch above the table.

"As high as it will go," said Henry, rising once more.

Emma eyed the contraption next to the book. It was about a

foot tall and looked a bit like a piece of navigation equipment. She noticed that there was a glass lens to look through at the top. "What is that device?" she asked.

"It is a microscope," said Henry.

"What is it for?" she asked.

Henry considered the question as he returned from his trunk with a stack of small objects. "It is a bit like Owen's spyglass," he said, "but for objects that are exceedingly near."

"Why would you need a spyglass for objects that are nearby?" asked Owen.

"Because those objects are exceedingly small," said Henry, handing each of the others a small object. "Careful, they are fragile," he said. "Glass."

Emma took hers carefully and looked at it. It was a small rectangle made of thin glass. "What are we to do with these?" she asked.

"Just a bit of spit, right in the center, please," said Henry.

He wants me to spit *on it?* thought Emma. This all seemed so strange. For a moment she thought she might be too nervous to work up any spit. Her mouth felt like cotton. She managed by thinking of her favorite food: a good duff pudding.

The others managed as well, though some with more accuracy than others.

"All right," said Henry. "Who's first?"

No one volunteered. Emma looked around and saw the

others holding their little squares of spit as if they were made of gold. *Maybe I should just get it over with*, she thought, but she couldn't bring herself to speak up. *What if it's me?* Inhaling deeply, she knew that she certainly didn't smell like perfume, but she had felt a bit clumsier than usual lately. She'd chalked it up to soreness and fatigue, but what if . . .

"Fine," said Henry. "I'll go first."

He held up one of the glass rectangles. "A slide," he said, then promptly spit on it. He wiped the edge with a bit of cloth and then placed another slide over the top of the first, sealing the gob in place in a sort of slide sandwich.

Emma watched with equal parts fascination and fear as he slid the slides onto the little platform near the base of the microscope. "What are you looking for?" she asked.

Henry had begun to bend down over the scope, but now he looked up, seemingly grateful for the delay. "I'm looking for any sign of fungal growth," he said. "The spores, of course, or perhaps some sort of fibrous growth."

Fibrous growth . . . The phrase both confused and scared Emma. In her mind, she pictured a poisonous bush.

Henry ignored her sour expression and continued. "I got the idea from the creatures themselves. The tongues of both were, well, *fuzzy*. The mouth seems to be a focal point for the infection—a good, moist breeding ground—as I am sure those white fibers are fungal in nature. I have seen their like before, growing upon the sides of fish."

Emma considered vomiting. Fortunately, Henry stopped talking and bent down over his microscope. The group seemed to hold its collective breath as Henry put his eye up to the lens. He was silent for a few long seconds. The seconds grew. Henry adjusted something on the scope.

"Well?" said Owen at last.

Henry looked up and blinked a few times. Then he broke into a smile. "Well, I am definitely in need of a good dental cleaning, but I see no signs of the organism."

This seemed to embolden the others, and suddenly everyone was holding out their slide for inspection. Everyone except Emma.

Henry reached out and plucked Owen's slide from his hand, bypassing both Thacher and Maria, who were closer. Something had changed between Henry and Owen, Emma realized. The two were more or less complete opposites and had instantly distrusted each other at the start of the voyage. But now? They seemed to share a sort of mutual respect. She would almost venture to call it friendship.

Trust, though, was in short supply. Henry had slipped a black glove onto his right hand to handle the saliva-strewn slides.

He carefully covered Owen's slide and placed it under the microscope.

Once again, Emma held her breath and stared. Suddenly, she felt something prodding into her side. She looked over to see Owen holding the pistol by its barrel and poking her with the handle.

"What on earth?"

"Just take it," he said. "In case it's me."

She nodded and took the gun from him, wrapping her hand around the smooth wood of its handle. If the fungus was in him—if it was in any of them—it was a death sentence. Who could say what desperate acts that might provoke? *But could I possibly shoot this boy?* She stole another glance. How could she put a lead ball between such perfect brown eyes?

She could only hope she wouldn't have to. Once again, they all turned to Henry, who was already bent over his work. "Hmmm," he said, and just as everyone was parsing the sound of it—*was that a good "hmmm" or a bad "hmmm"?*—he looked up brightly.

"You can give him his gun back, Emma."

There was a collective exhale. As she gave Owen his gun back, she realized the real reason Henry had chosen Owen first. He would be the enforcer. They had both been cleared. Now Henry could serve as the judge, with Owen, at least potentially, as the executioner.

Maria was up next.

Emma said a silent prayer. *Please, dear Lord, not her.*

It wasn't. As Emma crossed herself, Thacher was already handing over his slide.

"And what if I fail?" he asked.

Henry took the slide with his gloved hand and said flatly, "Then you are already dead."

The words went off like a cannon in Emma's mind as Henry pressed his eye up to the lens. Emma watched with the others, but she already felt alone. She still clutched her slide tightly in one hand, the thin glass edges threatening to add blood to the little island of spit at its center.

She looked over at Thacher. He was standing straight and still, his mouth pressed flat and his eyes shut, as if he were standing on the gallows about to be hanged. It occurred to her with a certain horror that Henry could say anything he wanted. No one else would know what to look for, or even how to look. She watched him fiddle with the top of the tube, adjusting some sensitive mechanism or other.

The two boys had never gotten along, she thought, and now Thacher's life was in Henry's black-gloved hand . . .

Henry looked up abruptly and stared at Thacher. Finding his eyes closed, he called his name: "Thacher!"

Thacher flinched visibly but opened his eyes. "What did you see?" he whispered, and Emma was almost touched by the amount of faith he seemed to have in the strange device.

"I'm a bit concerned," Henry began, causing the others to

take a step back from Thacher. "It looks like your gums are bleeding, and it could be a sign of scurvy."

Thacher snorted out a laugh and then said, "There's plenty of fruit in Cuba."

"That was cruel," said Maria.

Henry hadn't been able to resist a bit of revenge after all, but he pretended not to know what she was talking about. "Emma?" he said.

Emma's heart was pounding so hard that it seemed as if it was trying to escape her chest. Her hand shook visibly under the bright light as she extended her slide toward Henry. She was relieved when he took it quickly, but once he had it, she didn't know what to do with herself. Should she stand as Thacher had, braced for the fatal words?

A warm hand slipped slowly around hers. She looked over. It was her sister. The two would end this voyage as they had started it, shoulder to shoulder. Maria gave Emma's hand a quick squeeze and Emma squeezed back.

Suddenly, Henry looked up. He turned his head toward Emma, and she was the first to see the look in his eyes. *Is it astonishment or . . .*

"You are fine," he said, before widening his gaze to take in the rest of the crew. "We are all fine."

No, not astonishment, Emma realized. Relief.

Thacher started laughing out of pure joy and gratitude, and

the others joined in, acknowledging for the first time just how scared they'd truly been.

"Still one more crew mate to test," said Owen, who had corralled Daffy and now lifted the ship's cat onto the table. The laughter increased.

"How are we going to get any spit out of her?" said Thacher.

"Just wait a moment," said Owen, still holding her in place. "She'll hiss."

Instead, Henry rubbed a slide against Daffy's raspy cat tongue and cleared her too.

Emma laughed along with the others and gave Daffy a nice scratch behind the ears. There was still danger on board the *Polaris*, she knew, but that danger was lurking somewhere outside this cabin. It was danger from without and not from within.

That was the kind of danger they could fight. And looking around at this strange community they had built—this strange group that had fractured and somehow formed again—she knew they would do that fighting together.

CHAPTER 32

GIVING UP THE GHOST

Owen looked out over the bow one more time and saw the massive island of Cuba spreading across the horizon. It was long but still little more than a fuzzy green line in the distance. Now that they had finally decided to head for shore, the heavy, waterlogged ship was being maddeningly slow about getting there. Owen could practically hear its innards slosh back and forth as it rolled over the small coastal swells. Making matters worse, the current wanted to push them to the west and what wind there was seemed to agree.

I used to want that too, he thought.

"We'll have to come in at an angle!" he called back to Maria at the wheel.

She eyed him suspiciously.

"Yes, do it," called Emma from across the deck. "We'll cover more sea but still get there faster. Just a few points to the west."

Owen thanked Emma with a lift of his chin as Maria began to turn the ship. The others went about their tasks. During a lull in the wind, Owen heard a crash from within the cabin and winced. Thacher was ransacking it for anything valuable enough to sell and light enough to get through the waves to shore. *They would sell the family silver after all . . .*

The task should have been Owen's, but he couldn't bring himself to do it. Instead, he'd drawn the short straw and landed the job that should have belonged to the former powder monkey. He knelt back down and finished wrestling the barrel of gunpowder out of the shadowy interior of the low forecastle. He lugged it free and then began rolling it carefully across the unstable deck. The mutineers had tried to blow up the ship once, and they had failed. Owen himself had helped see to that. The idea of completing their work cast a shadow over his thoughts.

He rolled the barrel up against the mainmast and lashed it in place. Then he took out his knife and began carving a small hole in the top for the fuse. Once he'd finished, he looked up at the sawed-off end of the port-side mainsail yard. It felt like a lifetime ago that the thing had cracked. He felt a sudden, almost crushing tenderness for the *Polaris*.

Any sailor will tell you that a ship has a soul. The give of the wood, the creak of the metal, the whistling of the ropes, and the snap of the canvas—even the way it rides across the waves . . . At times it can seem more alive than any single member of the crew.

And now, he thought, dropping his eyes, *we are going to blow it to smithereens.*

He pressed his palm against the warm wood of the mast for

just a moment. Then he straightened up and went to get a length of fuse from the gun locker. As he did, he crossed paths with Emma, who was on her way to the toolshed.

"Time for the saw," she said.

Owen nodded solemnly. Before they could blow up the ship, they still had to subject her to a few last indignities.

Next, he passed Henry, who was cutting up old sailcloth to make a sturdy sack to hold their valuables and necessities in the water. In addition to attempting to blow her up, the mutineers had also robbed the *Polaris* of her last boat. Now the young crew would have to improvise to get to shore. It would not be a dry journey.

He crossed the quarterdeck and braced himself for what he was about to see as he pushed open the door to the cabin. Sure enough, Thacher had turned the place upside down in his quest for loot. Owen shook his head sadly as Thacher dropped another handful of trinkets onto a growing pile in the center of the table.

"Don't forget the navigation equipment," Owen said glumly. "Valuable and easy to sell."

"Oh, yes! Thanks!" said Thacher with a bit of greedy glee in his voice.

Owen searched through the gun locker. The guns themselves had been lost to the mutiny, and the cannonballs, powder, and such were mostly kept below deck. But he knew that some spare cordage was always kept in the locker—it was, after all, the single driest place on board the ship. He found a coil of thick black fuse slumbering like a serpent on the bottom shelf and began unspooling some.

"A goodly length, please," said Thacher. "We will want some time."

Owen shrugged. "How much time will it take to jump overboard?"

Thacher released a small, surprising chuckle.

"I brought the sack," said Henry, appearing at the door.

And as he did, a chill shot through Owen. He had a bad feeling about all of this. It wasn't a feeling of sadness this time but of danger. At first, he didn't understand it, and then he did. They were standing around, chatting amiably, not moving with any real urgency, not watching their backs. And with three of them in the cabin, they had left only two on deck.

The next sound he heard was the splintering crack of wood.

"Oh no!" he breathed.

With four feet of curling fuse in one hand and his pistol in the other, he rushed toward the deck, praying he was not already too late.

Emma was standing on the bulwark, trying to figure out how to swing herself up into the rigging with a heavy saw in one hand, when she heard the wood begin to shatter. The sound was coming from the forecastle this time, and she swung her head that way.

The forward hatch, she realized. The one without the spikes and nails.

She watched as it was obliterated by a brutal assault from below. There were two quick blows, and with each, the boards bent and broke and pulled free of their moorings. Then a third, stronger blow, and the boards all but exploded outward. A black gap appeared at the center of the hatch, and the creature's gruesome head pushed upward into the sunlight. Obed's face in its dark red helmet peered out from under two bobbing antennas.

She gasped as his eyes—blood-red where they had once been white—locked onto hers. Suddenly, a scream. *Maria, no!* thought Emma, but it was too late. Obed's eyes swung around and stared down the deck at the hobbled sister at the helm.

"Get out of there!" Emma yelled as the creature launched itself up out of its hole and across the deck. All six legs, fully grown and formed now, tore across the wooden deck in a skittering, off-balance run. It was a fast but rhythmless gallop that made Emma queasy.

"Maria, please!" she called back. Finally tearing her eyes free from the mesmerizing horror she turned to look for her sister. Instead, she heard the cabin door slam open and saw Owen rush out onto the deck. He was running at full speed toward the racing creature. The giant insectoid adjusted its course, away from the wheel and toward the boy. They would collide in seconds. Emma held her breath. The monster rose up, lifting its front legs like battle-axes as it raced forward on the other four.

Owen fired. A sharp crack and a cloud of smoke.

Emma watched the beast, hoping to see it crumple to the deck. Instead—*ping!*—the lead ball ricocheted off the thick armor plating of its thorax. She heard the deflected projectile whistle past her, just a few feet from her head, and smelled its burn in the salty air.

The creature brought its forelimbs down, splintering the wood where Owen had just been. Through the clearing smoke, Emma saw him tumble toward the rail in a heavy, thumping somersault. He rose as the creature pivoted toward him, bending from its strangely thin waist and rising onto its hind legs, towering above him. Owen responded by flinging the empty pistol at it like a tomahawk.

Surprisingly, his aim was much better with the weapon empty. The butt of the pistol smacked heavily into what had once been Obed's forehead. The creature staggered backward, and Owen made the most of the opportunity. He vaulted onto the top rope of the railing and from there scrambled easily into the ratlines.

The creature recovered quickly, but Owen was already well out of reach. It released an angry hiss, showing its fuzzy white tongue to the sky. The creature wheeled back toward the helm, but Maria, mercifully, had already managed to drag herself up into the rigging on the other side.

Emma took a long overdue breath and, having looped the saw handle through her rope belt, began to climb herself. She was sure the armor-plated creature was too heavy to climb these ropes, and that its barbed feet would cut through them regardless.

The creature seemed to realize this too. Rising to its full height, it raged at them all. Its hideous hissing was an utterly inhuman sound, and yet somehow it issued forth from the chapped lips of a boyish face.

And then, with profoundly awful timing, Henry and Thacher poked their heads out of the cabin to see what was going on. "No, go back!" called Owen, but it was too late. The creature swung around instantly and began charging toward the door. From her place alongside the mainmast, Emma heard Henry say something like "EEEEP!"

She watched as the two boys retreated, slamming the cabin door behind them. But one look at the charging creature told her the door wasn't nearly thick enough. She watched in horror until a voice broke the spell. "Saw it down!" called Owen. "We can't help them from up here, and it won't take the thing long to realize it can bring down these masts!"

Emma nodded. He was right. She scampered up the ratlines and quickly reached the sprung mainsail yard. Owen had sawed off the end on the port side, and now she began sliding out along the still intact starboard side of the crossbeam. She pushed the heavy saw ahead of her as she went.

"Hurry, Emma!" called her sister, but her words were drowned out by the sound of splintering wood on the deck below.

No sooner had Henry and Thacher retreated into the cabin than the door—and really, the wall—had come crashing in after them. Henry raised one hand to cover his face and felt a thick splinter pierce the tender skin of his palm. Lowering his hand, he saw the top of the creature's head and realized it had rammed the door like a charging bull. He watched in horror as the creature raised its head.

Obed's eyes were crimson in the light from the back windows. Despite their monstrous framing, Henry saw something all too human in those eyes. *Anger*, he thought. *Accusation*.

"He knows," Henry whispered.

Thacher was too terrified to respond, but Henry needed no confirmation. The creature knew what they were doing— preparing to abandon the ship, to abandon *it*—and it meant to stop them. *How much of Obed is still in there?* he wondered again. *How much human intelligence is being made to serve a new master?* He was sure that the boy's brain was still in there, shot through with fungal fiber, infiltrated and harnessed. He remembered the Frenchman's scrawled reports of infected ants marching obediently to the center of their colonies before releasing their spores.

But the time for such academic thoughts was over. The creature stepped almost delicately through the hole it had just made. First one foot, then two, then three . . . Henry looked down. Only the little table was between the boys and the beast. It was made of thick wood and bolted solidly to the floor.

The boys held their breath and watched, as the creature stepped fully into the room and reached the front edge of the table. It wasn't that they were paralyzed with fear, exactly. It was more that they had nowhere left to go.

The creature pinned them in place with its blood-rimmed eyes. *Is that hunger I see there?* thought Henry. *Or something worse?*

It took a step around the left side of the table. Without a word but in perfect unison, Henry and Thacher both took a long step to the right. The creature turned the front left corner of the table, and the boys turned the back right corner. The creature paused. They paused.

Now the creature's mouth opened. Henry gazed at the patch of fibrous fungus inside and steeled himself for another of its hideous angry hisses. But nothing could have prepared him for what he heard instead.

Hehhhehhehh . . .

It was a breathy exhalation . . .

Hehhhehhehh . . .

It took Henry a moment to realize that the creature was laughing at them. It would not play this game. Instead, it placed one heavy barbed foot on top of the table, and then another. It began to pull itself up onto the table. Its exoskeleton had grown thick and heavy, and the wood strained under its weight but held. The boys took a half step back and then . . .

"Run!" yelled Thacher.

Run? thought Henry. *Run where?* They were only a few precious steps from the back wall, the back windows. *The windows! Of course!*

Henry wheeled around to find that Thacher was already one step ahead of him. He was bending down to pick up something from the cluttered cabin floor. Henry saw the ragged cloth of his shirt stretched tight against his back.

The creature saw it too. It crouched down on the tabletop and prepared to leap onto Thacher's exposed back, to pin him flat and finish him. But as its powerful legs began to push down—*KRICK!*—the little table split under the strain. Instead of flying forward onto its prey, the creature fell onto the floor, landing on its heavy ant-like posterior. The two sides of the split table flipped up and bookended it.

Thacher stood and heaved his own sea trunk through the bank of leaded glass windows. *Pa-KRIISH!* The trunk took out one of the windows almost entirely. Without so much as a look back, Thacher plucked the canvas sack of valuables from the floor, leaned forward, and dove straight through the empty frame.

A few last shards of glass tinkled to the floor as the creature's feet scrambled for purchase among the broken, shifting wood.

Henry rushed forward but not toward the window. Instead, he reached his own trunk and quickly flipped open the latches. He felt the creature's presence looming behind him, but he would not leave without this.

In the end, he discovered, he did have a responsibility to science—and a need to understand this organism. He reached into the corner of the trunk and pulled forth a small, soft shape. A jar wrapped carefully in wool.

A shadow fell across his back. He sensed the bulk of the creature and heard its hind feet scratch against the wood as it rose up behind him.

Henry spun around, whipping the scrap of blanket away as he did. As he fell back onto the floor, he lifted the jar. The movement caused the rat-creature inside to jostle and bounce, almost as if alive.

Gazing through the spore-frosted glass, Henry saw the creature looming above him, one powerful foot raised to deliver a crushing blow. But it hesitated and peered down at the mutated rat. Henry slowly rattled the jar again—it was easy to do with his hands shaking from fear.

Once again, the rat-creature shifted and shivered.

The creature lowered its head and looked more closely. Its barbed foot lowered slightly. *Surely*, thought Henry, *it would not harm one of its own.*

But he was wrong.

The creature let out a long and angry hiss and raised its murderous forelimb once more.

Henry realized too late: Of course, it would harm one of its own. What did he think it had been eating down there all this time?

As the creature clubbed one barbed limb down toward the floor, Henry pushed off with both legs and rolled to his left, doing his best to keep his arms rigid and shield the glass jar.

The creature missed Henry by inches, hammering the floor so hard that it punched a hole clear through it. Henry rolled again, closer to the window. He rose to one knee as the creature pulled its barbed forefoot from the splintered wood.

The creature gathered its hind legs underneath it as Henry gathered his own legs beneath him.

It leapt; he leapt.

Suddenly, sunlight. Henry was bathed in it as he cleared the empty windowpane. He heard a heavy crash of wood and glass behind him and braced himself for searing pain, for something to catch his foot and hold it fast.

But his feet were clear of the cabin now.

He felt his body begin to arc down toward the ocean.

They had both leapt at the same time, but the creature was far heavier.

Henry bent like an arrow at the end of its flight, descending toward the tropical blue sea.

A moment before he splashed down, he tossed the jar gently to one side. *It must not break now.* He heard its soft splash and felt the warm embrace of the Caribbean.

He dove down deep, testing himself for any pain in the sudden buoyancy. *Am I really still in one piece? Am I really still intact?*

He was.

He swam to the surface and blew out some salt water. He looked up to find Thacher a few feet away, floating alongside his trunk with the canvas sack slung across its top.

"Your rat's over there," he said.

Henry nodded his thanks and swam over to retrieve the floating jar—and the invaluable scientific specimen within. As he did, he cast one eye up toward the broken cabin windows. The ship was already two dozen yards on, still sailing slowly toward shore. But all he saw at its stern was an empty pane and a featureless darkness within.

He had to raise his eyes up to see the full story.

CHAPTER 33

SOUND AND FURY

Owen descended the rigging with reckless speed. The creature had disappeared into the wrecked cabin, and as worried as he was about Henry and Thacher, he needed to take advantage of the opportunity. He swung off the last ratline and dropped down cat-footed onto the gently rolling deck.

He landed in a crouch and peered back toward the cabin. He saw only shifting shadows through the jagged hole where the door had once been. Then he heard a sudden crash of breaking glass. He smiled, picturing the others diving headlong to the relative safety of the sea.

As he rose to his feet, he was already pulling the coiled fuse from his belt and measuring some out. He looked directly up the mainmast and saw Emma laying out on the yard, furiously sawing away at the wood. "Almost done?" he hollered.

Emma grunted and then shouted back: "Close!"

Owen looked down at the coiled black fuse in his hand. If he made it too short, he would blow the ship up while Emma was still aloft. If he made it too long, the creature might identify the

271

threat and extinguish it, just as it had splashed water on his pistol below deck. "How close?" he called back.

"Look out below!" she called down triumphantly.

A slow splintering sound gave way to a thunderous crack and suddenly the starboard end of the yardarm was plummeting toward the deck. Owen barely had time to cover his head before it hit. There was a huge hollow *BONK* as the sawed-off spar hit the side of the deck. The force of it bounced Owen off his feet and up into the air. Stunned by the impact, he landed on his backside just aft of the powder keg. The big wooden beam bounced up and toppled over the railing, landing in the water with a resounding splash.

The falling yard had torn some of the starboard rigging, and as Owen looked up, he saw Emma descending toward him on the port side. He gathered himself to rise to his feet.

Suddenly, he heard a skittering chorus of clicks and clacks from the forecastle. He turned toward the gaping hole in the forward hatch. The yardarm had beat the deck like an enormous drumstick, and it had stirred up something from deep in the hold. A dark red ratlike creature emerged from the hatch, then a second, and then they all began to pour out. One dozen, two dozen.

Two of Owen's least favorite things, rodents and insects, had merged perfectly—three of his least favorite things if you counted the fungus that had somehow glued them together.

And now a wave of them was streaming straight for him, their long black front teeth gnawing at the air.

Owen desperately scrambled to his feet, but he already knew he would never reach the rail in time. Would they gnaw him to death, or would they too seek to transform him?

Suddenly, they stopped, all but skidding to a halt. They formed a jagged line and hissed viciously, showing their sharp black teeth. *Why would they stop?* wondered Owen, finally reaching his feet. *Why would they threaten me with teeth that could already be sunk in my flesh?*

Then he heard another sound: a soft thud followed by a rasping scrape.

Oh no.

They hadn't stopped because of him. They had stopped because of what was behind him.

"Watch out!" called Emma from somewhere just up above.

By the time Owen turned his head, the creature was already rushing toward him with its strange fractured gallop. Owen took off at a run, straight toward the line of rats. He made it just a few steps before the creature's shadow fell across him. Reaching over, he grabbed the mainmast with both hands and swung himself up and around it. His sweat-slicked palms held on just long enough to whip him around to the other side.

The creature tried to stop, but its bulk was too great. It

skidded into the front line of rat-things, causing them to scatter in all directions.

With shaking hands, Owen snapped off a short length of fuse and managed to stuff it into the hole he'd carved in the top of the powder keg. He took the tinderbox from his vest pocket, but it was hard to use with shaking hands. He struck it awkwardly, and the weak spark failed to ignite the little pinch of rope fiber within. An armored rat scampered past his feet, but Owen had bigger problems. Much bigger. The creature's shadow fell over him once more as it rose up to its full height.

He shot a desperate look in its direction—and he saw a handsaw bounce off its back.

The creature hissed up into the rigging. The handle of a knife conked off its head. Emma and Maria were throwing everything they had down at the thing.

Owen turned back to the fuse. He exhaled, willing his trembling hands to obey him. He wouldn't get another chance. He struck flint against steel once more. A fat spark jumped from the steel and landed on the rope fiber. The pale strands began to glow red as he blew on them softly and held them to the fuse.

With a sputtering crack, the fuse caught fire. Owen leapt to the side as the cord began to hiss and pop. He felt a quick breeze as the creature's barbed forefoot passed just inches from his cheek. As he turned to run, he heard two quick splashes. The Spanish sisters had jumped overboard. He raced to join them.

He hopped over one mutant rat only to land just inches from another. He hopped again without breaking stride. This time he landed firmly on both feet and sank down to his knees in front of the sagging rope at the rail. He reached over to pluck one last thing from the edge of the deck. It squirmed wildly in his hands.

"Settle down, Daffy," he said. "This is for your own good."

Then, as the creature crashed toward them, Owen pushed down with both feet and jumped straight over the side of the ship.

He splashed down into the sea to the sound of cheering in the distance.

The warm water enveloped him. It felt good, but he knew he wasn't safe yet. He swam up and forward. As soon as he broke the surface, he began to swim away hard from the ship. With the soggy, deeply unhappy ship's cat under one arm, Owen was forced to use a sidestroke rather than the faster crawl. But the ship was moving too, still sailing steadily away, doubling the distance between them.

He kicked hard and took one last look back toward the *Polaris*. The creature was raging at him from just behind the rope railing. Its black-toothed mouth hissed, and its blood-rimmed eyes glared.

Owen had asked Henry, at the start of their final preparations, whether ants could swim. His answer then gave Owen comfort now. "Real ants are small enough to float for a bit, but the armor of this one is far too thick." Owen understood neither the biology nor the physics of it, but he smiled as he remembered Henry's next words: "It would sink like a stone."

He kicked away from the ship, and as the creature watched him go, something seemed to occur to it. It ceased its raging and spun its head around. It stared back toward the mast—and the keg at its base. Suddenly, it turned and disappeared from view.

Owen dove down below the waves, once again taking the squirming, disgruntled cat with him. The sound of the first explosion carried through the water, muffled but unmistakable. Then, almost immediately, there was a second and much larger blast as the main stores of gunpowder below deck went up. The explosion rang through Owen's entire body. The surface of the water above him turned a bright blood-orange. A moment later, chunks of wood began raining down.

He stayed under for as long as he dared, but not knowing how long a cat could hold her breath, he was forced to surface.

"Over here!" he heard over the sound of roaring flames.

He looked over to see an odd little flotilla. Emma, Maria, Henry, and Thacher were clinging to the yardarm, their hair slicked back by salt water and just their upper bodies visible. Henry was holding his jarred mutant, and Thacher had one arm on his trunk, which was floating alongside the yard and topped with the sack of valuables.

What an odd bunch, he thought, brimming with affection.

"Is that Daffy with you?" called Emma.

"It is," said Owen, swimming toward them. "And she is *not* happy."

"The ship is alight behind you," called Henry, as if Owen could possibly have missed that.

"I know it is," said Owen, but even once he had his own spot along the yard and Daffy was transferred safely to the top of the floating trunk, he didn't look back at it. He had no doubt it was a remarkable sight: flaming wreckage, sinking beneath the waves.

He had made up his mind, though. He would not look. That would not be his last view of the sailing ship that he had been so proud to call home.

Instead, he kept his eyes forward. He saw the white of the crashing waves off in the distance now, and the green of the fields beyond.

"What will happen to us?" said Maria.

"We will be all right," said Owen.

"But before you said—" began Henry.

"I know what I said," Owen cut in. "But I was wrong."

"Right, wrong, we all made mistakes," said Thacher. Owen knew that was as close as he'd get to an apology for the conk on the head, and it was good enough for him.

"And we have money," continued Thacher, "a whole sack of it."

"We have lost one of our own," said Emma, and the memory of poor, ever-cautious Aaron passed over them like a dark cloud above the glittering sea.

"But we still have each other," she added, and a bit of light broke through again.

Owen opened his mouth to respond, but what did he have to add, really? He nodded instead. They did have each other—a mismatched crew, perhaps, but capable and battle-tested. Who could outsail the sisters? Who could outthink Henry? And who, in their right mind, would want to meet Thacher in a dark alley?

And all of them—the survivors—continued to kick toward shore as the last of the shattered, smoldering remains of the *Polaris* sank slowly behind them. Soon, the sound of crashing waves mixed with the calls of shorebirds.

Then a third sound mixed in. Human voices. Owen looked up and saw them on the beach, little figures, still small in the distance. He felt his nerves swell along with the rolling wave that lifted the yard beneath him. Then, as the wave passed, he heard himself laugh. He was being ridiculous again.

What does it matter if we wash up on a foreign shore? The U.S. was just a thin island and a narrow strait away now.

And how can we be scared of mere men when we have overcome monsters?

AUTHOR'S NOTE

This is a work of historical science fiction. A few liberties have been taken with the ship and the sailing, for example (though I daresay you'd have to be a real old salt to spot them). Most of the science in this fiction, however, is biological. It is about living things, not machines.

The creature in the book is based on a real species: *Ophiocordyceps unilateralis*, the infamous "zombie bug" fungus of the Amazon. It really does infect ants' brains and direct them to march into the center of their colonies. Then it blooms *from their heads*, spreading its deadly spores. And it is true that parasitic funguses—and this one, in particular—sometimes jump between species.

Ophiocordyceps was discovered in 1859 by Alfred Russel Wallace, a major British naturalist who discovered all kinds of things. I simply speculated that this fascinating fungus might have been noticed a bit earlier—and then taken a very dark turn in its development.

The 1830s really were a time of tremendous scientific discovery and exploration. That was made possible by sailing ships and their brave crews, including many ship's boys (and no doubt a few ship's girls). The HMS *Beagle* is the most famous of those vessels. It set sail in 1831 carrying a young naturalist named Charles Darwin. Not all scientific discoveries are happy ones, though. *Polaris* is a story about what might have been.

—MN